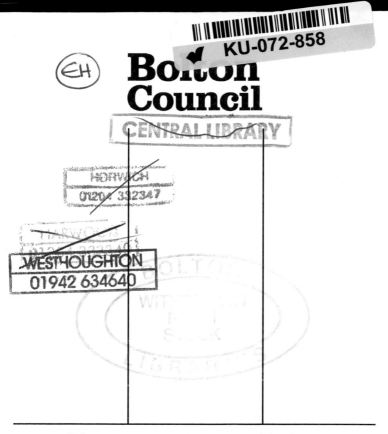

Please return / renew this item
by the last date shown.
Books may also be renewed by
phone or the Internet.

Tel: 01204 332384

www.bolton.gov.uk/libraries

Chace Hexx

At the age of twenty-eight, Chace Hexx is in danger of letting life pass him by. Drifting from ranch to ranch, he hones his skills with guns, horses and cattle, but to what purpose? Then, out of the blue, a proposition is made by a friend who turns out to be something rather different. Gunplay, tragedy, murder and disaster suddenly give Chace a new purpose in life. Vengeance is sweet, but the most dangerous task still lies ahead. All his skills are going to be needed searching from Arizona to Colorado, where he falls for a pretty young widow who adds a whole new bunch of problems to his overburdened shoulders. Is there no end to it?

Chace Hexx

Frank Chandler

A Black Horse Western

ROBERT HALE

© Frank Chandler 2018
First published in Great Britain 2018

ISBN 978-0-7198-2796-9

The Crowood Press
The Stable Block
Crowood Lane
Ramsbury
Marlborough
Wiltshire SN8 2HR

www.bhwesterns.com

Robert Hale is an imprint
of The Crowood Press

The right of Frank Chandler to be identified as
author of this work has been asserted by him
in accordance with the Copyright, Designs and
Patents Act 1988

Typeset by
Derek Doyle & Associates, Shaw Heath
Printed and bound in Great Britain by
4Bind Ltd, Stevenage, SG1 2XT

1

Chace Hexx was perched on the livery-yard fence. There was a distant glaze across his eyes. A plug of tobacco sat in his hand, but his mind wasn't focused. Although the corral rail was not physically uncomfortable to sit on, after a year of casual work at the livery, Chace knew it was time to make a move. He rolled the tobacco into a paper and struck a match on his boot. Flies buzzed round his head. It was late summer, but the afternoon sun was still hot on his back. He blew a stream of smoke into the air. He was dreaming of lush green pasture a million miles from dry and dusty Arizona, being grazed by a herd of beef – his own verdant pasture and his own fine beeves. The smoke swirled and disappeared, and the dream with it. Trouble was, he'd slipped into a lazy life. The livery wages were nothing to shout about, nothing that was going to be enough to turn dreams into reality, but board and lodging was all in, and a kind of lethargy had settled on him. At twenty-eight, he was literally on the fence between having an easy time and feeling he should make something of his life. And there was an attraction in staying at the livery: Roseanne, the livery owner's daughter, brightened anybody's day with her disarming smile, gleaming chestnut hair and happy disposition. She was just twenty-one and had plenty of admirers in the town. Chace hadn't promoted himself to Roseanne and there was nothing romantic between them, but he wished there might be.

Roseanne was calling him. 'Chace! Chace Hexx!'

Over the years he'd drifted further and further westwards. Now he'd pitched up in Benton, a dreary sprawl of sun-baked town somewhere west of the line separating the territories of Arizona and New Mexico. Benton had started life as nothing more than a shamble of low timber supply buildings serving the huge cattle industry that was spreading across the region. With growing prosperity the buildings in Main Street were acquiring tall false fronts and fancy signs, although a couple of saloons did get a genuine second floor and call themselves hotels. Benton was developing into a small township.

Like many of the local cowboys and ranch hands, Chace found his entertainment in the saloons, but he was never tempted to join the hopeful fools, gambling away their last few dollars, stupidly trying to outwit the pasteboard artists cleverly dealing cards off the bottom of the deck. Chace could never fathom how these workers were so gullible. The year had passed quickly since he started working at the livery. It was a temporary job while he pondered his next move, but he felt no particular incentive to go somewhere else. In fact a kind of local plan was already forming in his mind. Maybe he'd pluck up the courage to find a way of becoming a partner in the livery – that way he might make enough money to buy a ranch. Benton Livery was a good business, and he got on well with

Roseanne. In any case, opportunities always drifted in and out of shanty towns, just as he had done himself. Something would turn up, and if he liked the look of it, he might be tempted.

'Chace! Where are you? I need your help.'

Roseanne was calling from the hay loft. Chace extinguished the end of his smoke and slid off the corral fence. He walked round the back of the barn. Roseanne was standing just off the top of the ladder, arms akimbo, one leg planted firmly on a golden bale. Even in the shadows of the hay loft, her chestnut hair gleamed and her hazel eyes sparkled. But her posture was a clear indication that Chace was about to be given a task.

'Yeah?' Chace replied, off hand.

Roseanne frowned at Chace's nonchalance. 'Come up here, can you?'

He climbed the ladder. 'I suppose you want me to move all those bales down to the barn?'

She nodded, smiled at him, and began to descend the ladder. She paused half-way down and looked up. 'It'll keep you occupied, for a while anyway, Mr Drifter.'

Chace laughed, and watched her complete her descent. Drifting was one thing, taking orders from such a young woman, however much she flashed her sparkling eyes at him, was quite another. It gave Chace a thrill when she turned her attention on him, but at the same time, her playful use of 'Mr Drifter' cut him more than she knew. He didn't need reminding.

In the little town in Georgia where he had spent a carefree childhood, Chace, like any young lad, had always been wary of the attractions of the opposite sex. That was until the soldiers started arriving from all directions. There'd been grey uniforms one day, dark blue uniforms the next. Then a hotch-potch of men in every-day wear with all kinds of strange get-ups, so you couldn't tell which side they were on. In a matter of weeks, his young life had changed from happy-go-lucky do-as-you-please, to a nightmare of fear and loathing. Whatever the uniform's colour, or even if there was no uniform at all, a child's eyes cannot forget witnessed atrocities.

In the final year of the war, at the age of seventeen, Chace had signed up for General Lee. His part in the endgame gave him three things: skill on a horse, a taste for guns, and a legacy of horrific nightmares. He blanked out other memories, preferring not to recall the things that happened in those months before the treaties were signed, but his life was changed forever.

Going home after the ignominy of Confederate defeat, he stared at the blackened carcass of a forgotten childhood. Confronting the disaster of a war-shattered town, littered with destroyed lives and dead relatives, he regretted ever going back. He had found practically nothing in the burnt-out shell of his own home, except an ash-heap of memories.

Without a backward glance, he had mounted up and ridden out. From that moment on, he had drifted further and further west, sinking deeper and deeper into a pointless life of occasional work, punctuated by bouts of depression. Nothing changed. Occasionally he would dream that everything was as it used to be, a happy home, a happy childhood. But on waking it all evaporated. More usually he had recurring nightmares of being over-run by hordes of dark-blue uniforms, dreaming his Enfield rifle had turned into a useless hayfork. He would thrust and parry but was stabbed so many times with bayonets, and shot through with screaming balls of hot lead, that he would wake in a cold sweat with a stinging sensation in his arms and legs.

Being skilled on a horse and handy with a gun, Chace found work easily as an itinerant cowhand. But the life was hard and seasonal, and he made few friends, always preferring to keep himself to himself. For that reason, he was never popular. He frequently moved on for a change of scenery and to escape the disdain of his fellows. He never looked back. For entertainment he drank occasionally, and he did sometimes play cards, like any other cowhand – but he was too intelligent to be sucked into a life of drunkenness and gambling. All these jumbled memories frequently haunted him, but hard physical work at Benton Livery prevented him dwelling on the past. He knew something better would turn up. Perhaps this would be the day.

As he was swinging another bale towards the hoist he could hear voices down in the yard. He recognized them: it was Roseanne talking to a cowpoke by the name of Tom Purdy. Tom worked out at the Crossed C's ranch, a big spread a few miles south of Benton. He was a frequent visitor to the livery and spent a lot of time gossiping with Roseanne, as did so many of the male visitors to the livery. Chace had enjoyed a few evenings with Tom in the saloon.

'He's round here in the hay loft,' Roseanne was saying. 'I hope you're not going to try and lure him away, Tom. We need him here. He's a good worker. He's strong, and does pretty much anything I say without question.'

Tom laughed. 'Show me a man who wouldn't!'

Roseanne blushed to the roots of her hair. 'Don't you tease me, Tom Purdy!'

'Isn't it time you chose a man to marry?' Tom insisted, with playful humour. He caught Roseanne by the arm and smiled. 'You know everyone loves you to bits.'

'I know,' she agreed. 'You're all butter in a hot frying pan.'

'Trouble is, we're a bit short-handed on the ranch. We need more men who are used to dealing with cattle. I think Chace might have that skill.'

Roseanne waved her arm in a defiant gesture. 'Well, it'll cost you if you take him away. Pa won't give him up without something in return.'

They had reached the ladder and Chace's interest in their conversation was growing. Roseanne called up to him. 'Chace, there's someone wants to see you.'

'Can I come up?' Tom asked.

Chace nodded. Tom climbed up and Roseanne left them to it.

Tom guided Chace into the very back of the loft and spoke in a hushed voice. 'I have a feeling you might have experience as a cowhand, am I right?'

Chace hesitated. He stared for a moment into Tom's deep blue eyes. They were sincere, without guile, friendly. Chace was intrigued. 'Maybe.'

'Can you handle a gun? Well, I know you can. Let's not whistle in the wind. Rosie told me you've got a six-gun and a rifle in your bunkhouse. I'm taking a chance talking to you like this, Chace. Each time I've come into the livery I've been watching you, and we've got to know each other quite well . . .'

'Yes, we have . . .'

'I'm a pretty good judge of character and I think I can trust you.'

'Trust me?' Chace repeated, puzzled. 'To do what?'

'Stand on the right side of the law, for one thing.'

'And for another?'

Tom paused and drew a deep breath. 'Bring a vicious gang to justice.'

'What?' Chace wondered, with incredulity. 'Part of a posse?' He paused, but Tom remained silent. 'You don't mean just us?'

Tom nodded his head slowly.

Chace was bewildered. 'But you're working out at Mr Winthrop's ranch, aren't you?'

'I am,' said Tom, 'but I've been biding my time as a cowboy waiting for the right moment to make my move.'

'And I'm guessing that means now.'

Tom held up his hand. 'Keep your voice down, Chace. There are ears everywhere.'

'You don't mean Roseanne and her pa?'

'No, of course not, but what people don't know they can't repeat. What I'm about to tell you mustn't go any further. Now listen up good.'

Tom laid it out for Chace.

'Mr Winthrop owns a lot of Benton like it's his property. He's provided it with the sheriff's office, the general store, the saloon, the church and the sidewalks. He pays the sheriff's wages, and sometimes stands us for drinks on the house in one of the saloons. He's a wealthy benefactor with a thriving cattle business and deep pockets. His cowhands drink in the saloons, gamble in the saloons, tumble the barmaids in the saloons, and spend their money in the town. They cause little trouble because Winthrop doesn't want any attention drawn to his Crossed C's ranch. But it's not all above board. A lot of the cattle is rustled. But that's not my concern right now. I've finally tracked down part of

11

a gang who are hiding at the ranch. They're outlaws, not cowpokes. It's a good hiding place. Everyone knows they're on the dodge, and now they're planning a big bank raid.'

'And we're going to stop them?'

Tom nodded. 'I had a ranch in north Texas, built up from almost nothing. Then one night some men took me by surprise. I was coshed, tied, and bundled away. I was released a few days later, shaken and bruised. When I got back to my ranch, all the cattle had disappeared. I guess they were quickly sold on east into the meat market or traded with other dishonest ranchers. I lost everything. I've been on the trail of this gang for a couple of years, always just behind them. They left a string of thefts, murder, bank raids and mayhem in their wake, and eventually I found their hideout.

'The core of the gang were six men – two pairs of brothers, the Reeses and the Hagens, and two desperados, Heyman and Nickleson. They got wind that I was getting a posse to arrest them, and they split. I lost the Hagens, Bull and Bart, they went north, but the other four came here to Arizona. Eventually I tracked them down to Winthrop's ranch. So I signed on with Winthrop, easy enough as an experienced cowhand, but really I was looking for an opportunity to get those sons-ofbitches away, and take them back to Texas to stand trial.'

'And that's where I come in?' Chace presumed. 'But why take them back to Texas? Why not just dispose of them?'

'I can only act within the law. In any case, personal reasons. Now they're planning a bank raid.'

Chace was dubious. 'Even if we take them alive at a

bank raid, I don't fancy riding hundreds of miles looking after three dangerous men, just you and me to keep a lid on things. What about the sheriff, surely he'd help?'

'You're forgetting Winthrop pays his wages. He sure ain't going to do anything without Winthrop's permission, and Winthrop isn't going to hand over anyone he's protecting.'

'This is sounding more and more risky.'

Tom hadn't finished. 'And that still leaves the Hagens. I think they took off for Colorado, but that's just a hunch. I want these four first, then I can go after them. Will you help? Think it over and meet me tonight for a beer in Ben's Saloon.'

Chace stroked his chin and watched Tom go down the ladder and leave the yard. What was it that was driving Tom? He was a determined man. Chace stood still for a while, deep in thought.

'Can't hear much activity up there!' Roseanne called out from below.

Chace smiled to himself – no, brainwork doesn't make a whole lot of noise. He picked a bale up and threw it over the edge. It thudded down into the yard.

'Hey! You mind that, Chace Hexx!'

Chace pushed the batwings and scanned the room. Tom was sitting at a table with a couple of beers in front of him. He was looking hopeful. Chace sat down, took one of the glasses and drained it. He wiped his mouth with his sleeve, ready to speak. But it was Tom who spoke first.

'Keep your eyes on me, Chace, but look over my shoulder. Do you see that group of men, seven or eight

13

of them in the corner? They're all from Winthrop's. The two men sitting at the table are the Rees brothers, Kent with Bevan on his right. Standing immediately behind them is Heyman, the lanky goof with the red necktie.'

'Aren't you taking a mighty big chance working in the same place as them? What if they recognize you? They must have seen you when they stole your cattle and kidnapped you.'

'I had a big moustache and longer hair then,' said Tom, with a deadly serious expression. 'Of course there are risks. I'm up against four ruthless and determined no-goods.'

'Four? Where's the other one?'

'Nickleson went missing a few days ago and I think he's gone to stake out their next target, DeSoto's bank in Platt's Cut. I need to act quickly. Are you in?'

Chace shrugged. It was impossible to say no.

The next day, wondering what he had signed up to, Chace took an early morning ride away from the livery out into the Arizona desert. He gathered some brushwood and lit a fire. He boiled some water in a tin can. Gently crushing some roasted coffee beans between two stones, a wonderful aroma immediately hit his senses and the world was suddenly a better place. Chace leaned back on his rocky seat while the coffee brewed. Pulling lazily on his tobacco, he blew a thin wisp of smoke into the cold morning air.

He was suddenly startled by a prairie falcon flying low and fast along the ridge, swooping within a few feet of his head. It wove its way between cactus and yucca, little more than a man's height above the ground, searching for an early morning meal. It gave no warning of its presence, it was there and gone so quickly. The quintessential raider.

Now the sunlight was spreading fast across the desert and in the silence of the morning Chace could hear life beginning to stir. He was feeling more positive about Tom's proposal. Perhaps at last he'd do something really worthwhile. The only thing bothering him was that he'd been seen with Tom in the saloon, and that might have been noticed by the Rees brothers. He kicked out the fire and rode back to the livery.

Roseanne was in the stable yard. 'You were up mighty early, Chace. Something eating you?'

'Just couldn't sleep so good, and didn't want to wake anybody else so I took off for a smoke.'

Later that morning Tom rode into the livery. Chace saddled up and they rode off together for a while in silence, then Chace turned to Tom with a serious face.

'You know,' he began, 'I've been doin' some thinkin'.'

'Reckon you have,' said Tom, 'you've got that kinda face on.'

'Yeah, I guess that's why I couldn't sleep. Why are you doing this, Tom?'

'I'm just a one-time cattle rancher ruined by some no-good sonsofbitches who stole my herd and my money. What these people do isn't just against the law, it's against law-abiding folk, like you and me. I was tryin' to make a decent living after the war, and I've never known anything besides hard graft. It don't seem right for a bunch of saddle tramps just to take everything I've worked for. I've got nothing now.'

Chace stayed silent because he knew Tom hadn't finished.

'I have to put a stop to people like these outlaws. They're the worst kind of thief. They destroy people's lives, ruin dreams, and are against everything this country stands for – opportunity, hard work and the rule of law. And there's a reward for bringing them in. That way I get something back so I can start over.'

Chace wanted to probe, but changed the subject. He said, 'I'd like to have a ranch of my own and raise some beef. I've worked enough ranches to know just about enough. . . .'

'And have some thieves come along and steal them in the night,' Tom said disdainfully. 'And take everything you worked for?'

'I'd shoot their balls off!'

'Well, that sounds fine and dandy, but it ain't that easy to catch clever thieves. It's taken me near two years to catch up with these boys. And the Hagens are probably establishing their own illegal rackets wherever they are. It never ends, but we must do what we can.'

'But I know so much about cattle rearing. I learnt good when I worked the drives.'

'Reckon you do. You're a dark horse, Chace Hexx. You don't give much away, do you?'

'You're a dark horse, yourself, Tom Purdy. There's more to you than you're letting on.'

Tom side-stepped. 'I guess you haven't got the money to get yourself a spread yet.'

'No,' Chace replied. 'Not yet. You got any ideas?'

'If you help me good, you'll have a share of the reward money.'

Chace pulled up sharp and looked Tom in the eye. 'Tom, I haven't known you for long, and we seem to get along fine, but I'm worried that . . .'

'Listen, if we pull this off, you can move away from here and get yourself a spread.'

Chace immediately thought of Roseanne. A vision of the future flashed across his mind's eye. They rode on in silence for a while.

Tom encouraged again. 'What do you think of that?'

Chace chewed on it for a moment. 'Sounds all well an' good. But are you sure we can take the Reeses and the other two during a bank raid?'

Tom turned sharply. He blew out a deep breath of frustration. 'I'm sorry, Chace. Maybe I'm getting carried away. I've finally caught up with these men after two years of trailing. I'm lucky none of them have recognized me. At least, I don't think they have.' He ran his hand across his top lip. 'I told you I had a big moustache before. I don't look quite the same, and it was night time when the four of them jumped me.'

Chace wasn't convinced. 'Listen,' he said, decisively. 'I don't know what kind of scrape you're getting me into, but now I can see it more clearly, it's getting mighty risky. I was all fired up with some high-falutin' idea of fighting for law and order. But I don't want to get shot up. I'm dreaming of somewhere that's green and lush, where the grass grows long and straight, where there ain't no cactuses or damn rattlers. Open spaces where a man can breathe fresh air, raise some beef and ride all day without being seared like a steak.'

'Just a dream,' Tom said.

Chace was undeterred. 'Maybe. You've got to have dreams, you said so yourself. And I don't want to be watching over my shoulder for disgruntled outlaws seeking revenge. You said there were four of them jumped you.'

'Yes, the Rees boys, Heyman and Nickleson. He stole my . . .' He stopped mid-sentence. 'I don't know where

17

Nickleson is. But staking out the biggest bank in Platt's Cut is my guess.'

Riding back into Benton, eddies of dry, dusty wind swirled along Main Street and the sun was hot on their backs. They hitched at the livery. Chace said he was going to see if Rosie was around. Tom went to the saloon to line up some beers. But everything was about to go haywire.

2

Chace reflected on the strange turn of events. Had he really signed up for what seemed like bounty hunting? It was true he had been waiting for something to turn up, but he hardly expected it to be like this. Was Tom Purdy really just a rancher chasing down some rustlers? The story about having his cattle stolen had the ring of truth about it. But would a rancher really travel hundreds of miles and spend two years trying to find the criminals? The thing that bothered Chace a lot was that Benton was owned and subsidized by Winthrop. The townspeople, however reluctant, would be sure to support Winthrop's employees against any accuser who hadn't got the backing of the law. Chace was beginning to wonder how he could get out of Tom's highly risky plan.

At the livery stable, Roseanne was seeing to a lame mustang cow-pony. She'd got the hoof between her legs and was carefully pulling out some prickly spines. The owner was standing next to her and watching. She deftly removed them one by one without breaking them off, which would have left the horse in a worse state. Eventually the last one was out and the horse seemed as pleased as the owner. Chace stepped forward.

19

'Chace!' Roseanne said flicking back her hair, her eyes lighting up. 'I didn't see you standing there.'

'Hello, Rosie. I was just quietly watching a horse doctor at work.'

'I'm no horse doctor,' she said. 'Just pulling a few nasty cactus spines.'

Chace put his hand on her shoulder. 'You got a minute to spare?'

'Sure.'

He steered her through the shed and out towards the corral at the back. She hopped up onto a rail and sat there with the sun glistening on her chestnut hair. She brushed it out of her eyes. He liked to watch her doing that.

'What's on your mind?' she asked straight out. 'Must be something big, I can tell.'

Chace exhaled a chuckle. 'A woman's intuition, I guess.' Then his mood changed to a more serious note. 'I'm thinking of buying me a spread and some beeves.'

'What's brought that on?' she laughed, furrowing her brow. 'There isn't much land round here that isn't already owned.'

'No, not here. Up north. A long way away. I want to settle down and make something of my life. I was wondering if. . . .'

'If I'd go with you?' she said, directly.

Chace was taken aback, it was almost as if she had known what he was going to say. 'Kind of.'

'What do you mean, "kind of"? I know what you're thinking.'

Chace hesitated, he was embarrassed at being so transparent. He scuffed the dirt with the toe of his boot. 'I know we haven't known each other all that long, but I always felt there could be something between us. I guess I never had the courage to say anything before, and . . .'

Roseanne cut him short. 'That's real sweet of you Chace, an' you know I'm fond on you, I like you a lot, but I couldn't leave my pa, not on his own to manage this place. All our energy has gone into building this business, and since ma passed on I don't want to run out on him just when things are looking up. I don't know how he'd manage on his own.'

'No, I guess not. I had a feeling that might be your answer. Anyway, I'm not really the marrying kind. . . .'

'Marrying? Was that a proposal, Chace Hexx?'

He was quick to cover his tracks, he hadn't meant it to sound like that, 'No, Rosie, I guess not. It's just part of a silly dream.' But he was bitterly disappointed that she hadn't shown more interest in going with him. 'Tom's got me a beer, so I'll cut along to the saloon and see you later.'

'Sure thing, Chace. Don't give up on your dreams. There'll be a girl waiting for you somewhere.'

He walked slowly back down the street to the saloon. The meeting with Roseanne had gone all wrong. It made him seem like he was needing a girl or a wife. It wasn't like that. Now he was wrestling with two emotions. He was real sore Roseanne had turned him down, but it made him more determined to leave Arizona for good. He'd have to help Tom, maybe get some reward dollars – there was nothing to lose.

He pushed through the batwings and stopped dead in his tracks. Tom was standing against the wall, his hands high over his head while his six-gun was being lifted out of its holster. Chace quickly looked to the barkeep, who shook his head to indicate he had no idea what was going on.

An eerie stillness had descended on the whole saloon as the assembled company watched in surprise. Card games had stopped, glasses had been put down, conversation had halted mid-sentence. Despite the increasingly mixed community of grafters and less honest characters, the expanding township of Benton was not yet noted for saloon brawls or rowdy behaviour before nightfall. Even then the sheriff kept a tight rein on gambling and merry-making. So what was going on here?

Chace scanned the scene and quickly realized that the young man taking Tom's gun and wielding his own Colt, was apparently acting with some kind of legal jurisdiction. He was proposing to take Tom into custody as a cattle rustler. He was saying out loud he'd been on Tom's trail for weeks.

'This here Tom Purdy is a wanted man in Texas, which is where I am going to take him.' So saying he turned the lapel of his coat and showed a brass, circled, five-pointed star. 'Ranger Nickleson,' he announced.

'That's a lie,' said Tom, shaking his head. 'He ain't no ranger.'

A ranger? Had Chace been fed some kind of lies in case something like this happened? Was it a coincidence that Nickleson had just been named by Tom as one of the gang? Whom should he trust? Chace tried to read Tom's eyes. His instinct was to trust Tom – but what about the badge? It looked real enough.

The ranger let it be known he intended to deliver Tom to justice, and wouldn't hesitate to put a slug in anyone who tried to prevent this lawful arrest.

This accounted for the silence in the bar. No out-of-state lawman dared to come near Benton and expected to get away with his life. A peaceful town, yes mostly, but it held on to its own and wouldn't give up anyone under any circumstances. Texas Rangers were getting a reputation for tracking down their quarry however long it took. This young ranger was clearly intent on making a name for himself, but he'd chosen the wrong time and the wrong place. And if Tom was to be believed, he wasn't a ranger anyway.

Chace made a decision and he hoped it was the right one. Any sudden movement would spark gunplay and the outcome of that was unpredictable. Nickleson's Colt would make a mighty big hole in anything that was struck by one of its bullets. The biggest danger was to Tom, with the Colt inches from the back of his head.

Holding his hands slightly raised to show he wasn't going to make a sudden draw, Chace spoke up. 'Well, this is a pretty situation we got here.'

Nickleson turned towards the batwings. 'How so?'

'Well,' said Chace, 'that's my friend you've got there and he ain't leaving this town.'

'Is that right?' replied Nickleson.

Chace nodded slowly, 'Sure is, but we don't want no trouble here, so I'll give you a deal. Let him go, mount up and ride out alive, and you'll see another day. Or be foolish, keep hold of him and book yourself a plot in the Benton town cemetery. What d'you say?'

With almost a note of light-heartedness in his voice, Chace's sinews were tightening like steel hawsers, but his nerves stayed ice cold. Whatever he did, he mustn't let that Colt go off.

Nickleson licked his lips as he slowly manoeuvred Tom towards the saloon's rear door, knowing that up to this point he'd been able to carry out his arrest with the element of surprise and bravado. He hadn't figured on

Tom having a good Samaritan turn up. Keeping his back close to the wall and Tom in front of him, Nickleson knew there was no scope for anyone to get a shot at him without the possibility of hitting Tom. If Nickleson was a gang member Tom must have been recognized and his number was up. This was a ruse to make it look lawful. Chace was thinking that he needed a diversion to distract Nickleson and get one clean shot at him.

Using eye contact with Tom, Chace let him know that at the crucial moment he should do his best to get down as low as possible. Then he looked to the barkeep and the bottle of whiskey on the counter. He flashed his eyes from one to the other, then to the floor and nodded. The barkeep nodded back to show the message was understood. Then Chace made one last appeal to the gunman.

'Look mister, we all admire your bravery. It took some guts to come in here on your own and arrest your man, and the last thing we want to do is put you six feet under. Nobody is going to take advantage of you if you just slide out that back door on your own and skidaddle.' Chace pointed to the bar. 'The barkeep'll even give you a bottle of whiskey to help you on your way.'

It was a clear signal, and the barkeep responded by chucking the whiskey bottle onto the floor towards the lawman who couldn't stop himself instinctively looking down at it. The bottle shattered. Chace went for his gun. At that exact moment, Tom jerked himself downwards enough to give Chace clear sight. Just one shot rang out, deafening everyone in the saloon and filling the room with acrid smoke.

Nickleson made a horrible, muffled, screaming noise of surprised agony as he slid down the wall, leaving a bright red streak marking his line of descent.

Chace took five dollars out of his pocket and said to the barkeep, 'Thanks, drinks all round.'

Tom was dusting himself down when the batwings flew open and the sheriff walked in.

'What in hell. . . .' he began. He walked over to the body slumped against the wall and leant down to feel the pulse. 'Not quite gone, but as good as. . . .' he said, closing the eyelids as the young man's spirit hesitated at the River Styx.

Brushing against the man's coat, the sheriff's expression suddenly changed. 'This here was a lawman, he's got a badge inside his lapel. A Texas Ranger.'

Several people spoke up at once pointing out that he'd grabbed Tom at gunpoint, never showed a badge, and was threatening to shoot anyone who stood in his way. They said he'd promised to put a slug in Tom if there was any trouble, and it looked as if he'd mistaken Chace's movement for a draw. Chace had simply responded in self defence.

'Well, I dunno about that,' said the sheriff. 'He was wearing a badge and that gave him the right. . . .' He touched his own five-pointed star as if to make it quite clear a badge of any sort should be a protection. 'When I've looked into this, Chace Hexx, I'll have to talk to Mr Winthrop and you may have to stand trial for killing a lawman.'

'That ain't no lawman,' Tom said casually. People expected him to say more, but he left it at that. He strode across to the batwings and walked out. Chace looked to the sheriff, shrugged and followed Tom. They walked back towards the livery yard.

Tom laughed, 'That's why Winthrop likes to keep a lid on things.'

'That man said something about you being wanted in Texas.'

'He would.'

Chace was puzzled. 'You said Nickleson was part of the gang, but he was wearing a badge. Was he really from Texas?'

'He was.'

'Was he Nickleson?' Chace asked.

'He was.'

Chace thought for a moment. 'Listen, Tom, I don't want to know any more than I have to, but you want my help and I have to trust you.'

Tom looked straight ahead. 'I knew him all right. I told you he was part of the gang, but I didn't know he was down here. When they jumped me, he stole my badge.'

'Why didn't you tell the sheriff?'

'And blow my cover at the ranch?'

'So you are a . . .'

Tom cut him short. 'Hush up!'

'Your cover must be blown if Nickleson was going to kill you.'

'Maybe,' Tom said dismissively. 'Anyways, how's Rosie?'

'Oh,' Chace said, immediately drawn back to his own predicament. 'She's all right,' he said, unable to hide the disappointment in his voice. He looked away to show Tom the conversation was closed. They walked back to the livery in silence.

3

The next morning Chace took his mug of hot coffee out into the livery yard, sat down on a log, rolled a smoke and watched Rosie at work. It didn't make him feel any better. Beautiful as she was, she now represented everything that was going wrong with his life. He started thinking. He didn't know if the sheriff had spoken with Mr Winthrop, or whether he was going to be arrested and stand trial. Even if Nickleson wasn't a lawman, the law in Benton did whatever Winthrop said. If Chace was really serious about getting out of this useless drifting life he was going to have to make the break soon. The feeling was becoming more urgent. He was still smarting from his hurt pride where Roseanne was concerned. It had been a foolish thing to approach her like that, and she was right to turn him down – but it hurt, nonetheless.

A moment later, Tom rode into the livery and walked into the yard. He wandered over and sat down with Chace. Chace wasted no time.

'Tom, you gotta come clean, was Nickleson a Texas Ranger?'

Tom raised his hands in a gesture of resignation. 'Never. He was a gang member, like I said. Truth is, I told you I thought he was staking out the bank.'

'If he was on to you, surely the rest of the gang know who you are.'

'Maybe. By the way, the talk at the ranch is that you were just a typical hot-head who acted against the law without thinking. Nobody is blaming you for what you did.'

'But it puts me at risk. I mean the Reeses might want to kill me for wasting their friend.'

'They've got bigger things on their mind. Now they're down to just them and Heyman. At least Nickleson is out of the way, that's one less to deal with. I haven't been quite straight with you and I apologize about that. I want to get them back to stand trial. We'll take the evidence that Nickleson's dead, too. There's a good reward for all four of them. Honest money.'

Chace was trying to take all this in when Tom lowered his voice to a whisper and continued, 'I've been watching them and listening to their conversations. The target is definitely DeSoto's Bank in Platt's Cut, twenty miles to the north of here.'

Chace sucked in a mouthful of air and blew it out slowly. 'Bank robbery always involves shooting and dead bodies. I'm not so sure I want any part of that. Why don't you just tell the sheriff in Platt's Cut? Why are you so keen to act on your own, or just with me? It don't make good sense.'

Just like after the Nickleson shooting, Tom wouldn't say any more about his reasons. 'Well, it's up to you, Chace, whether you're willing to help me or not. The Rees gang have killed innocent people while robbing banks. That's why I've been on their trail for two years. Rustling don't compare with cold-blooded murder.'

The news of the accident at Winthrop's ranch had spread quickly in the town. Chace left off his work the minute the news reached him, and went straight to the undertaker's. Standing beside the shroud, he turned back the top to look upon the horrible sight. He muttered a prayer. He only knew one verse, which he'd learnt from his Confederate prayer book: *Come near and bless us when we wake, Ere through the world our way we take, Till in the ocean of thy love, We lose ourselves in heaven above.* He said it from memory before every engagement with the Yankees, hoping to come out alive. He wasn't sure if it would do now for Tom, but finished with an 'amen' and hoped it was satisfactory.

A whole bundle of ideas raced around Chace's head. It now seemed obvious the Reeses or Heyman had recognized Tom, and realized he'd caught up with them. Nickleson's pretended arrest and intended disposal of Tom had been foiled by Chace. But this event wasn't an accident nor a coincidence. The official line was that the side of Tom's head had been kicked in by a horse – but horses don't kick that high. Everything that Tom had said about the gang was confirmed in his shattered skull, still wet with blood, covered with matted hair and exposing broken bone. Heads bleed a lot, and Tom's shirt down one side was soaked.

Chace went straight to the sheriff's office. He asked to look at Nickleson's badge, which was being held as evidence.

The sheriff took the badge out of a drawer. 'This is a Texas Ranger's badge,' he said. 'You shot a lawman, Chace Hexx.'

'Does it have anything on the back?' Chace wondered.

The sheriff looked closely. 'Yes, it does, a couple o' scratchy words.' He ran his thumb over the surface to shine it up. He squinted and said, '*Thomas Purdy*. Well I'm blowed. That ain't Nickleson, is it?'

'So, now you see. That wasn't a horse-kicking accident.' But Chace knew no action would be taken against anyone at Winthrop's ranch, and he didn't want to say anything about what he knew. 'Can I have the badge?'

'I guess it ain't no use to Thomas Purdy any more. And it puts you in the clear for the shooting, doesn't it?'

'He was a good friend,' Chace said. The badge was handed over and no further explanations were necessary.

Chace now feared for his own safety. For all he knew the gang might suspect that Tom had passed all his information to Chace, and he couldn't risk it. They might still be planning revenge for Nickleson's death. He had to act. Delay was impossible. He told Rosie and her pa why he had to go. For no good reason, he suddenly felt detached from the moment. Maybe it was the shock of Tom's death. Maybe the confirmation that Tom was a lawman. Maybe it was because Roseanne had turned him down. He seemed always to be losing. It was time to let it all go, and start over.

He took his gear out to the stable and saddled up his pinto. His few possessions fitted easily into the saddlebag. He slid his Winchester into the scabbard, secured his soogan behind the saddle, and attached his canvas bag to the pommel. He led his horse out into the yard, mounted, and with slight pressure from his heels and a clicking sound from his tongue, he rode quietly out of the livery yard for the last time. Roseanne watched him go, but he didn't turn round, he knew he dared not embed the memory.

Away from Benton, when the moon had gone over its highest point and the air was very cold, Chace found a suitable scrape to bed down. He hobbled the horse, unfurled his soogan, and looking up into the black night sky, drifted into a very deep sleep.

4

The shock of the previous day had taken its toll on Chace, and he slept beyond sun-up. It was the pinto moving about which finally woke him. He was up and ready to decamp in a very short space of time. He was sorry to have left the livery, but not sorry to be leaving Benton. In a strange turn of events this was exactly what he needed – a new and worthwhile purpose in life. His friendship with Tom Purdy had been short-lived, measured in weeks rather than months, but it had left Chace no alternative but to avenge his death and bring the perpetrators to justice.

There was no doubt the gang was ruthless, the evidence pointed to that. A Texas Ranger doesn't track outlaws like that for two years unless they are a scourge on society. Now they were planning another bank raid while hiding under the cover of Winthrop's ranch. Maybe there was something personal, too, for Tom. He had said they'd stolen something precious, and he wouldn't have meant the badge or the beef. Maybe a wife. Chace would never know. All that mattered now was to bring the gang to justice.

The scrubby country dotted with yucca, cactus, creosote, juniper and other low-lying prickly vegetation eventually gave way to sparse clumps of tough, grey needle grasses and a smattering of tree-clump cover. Thinking of nothing in particular, Chace was vaguely aware that his brain was working on a plan. Making his way to Platt's Cut he was subconsciously gathering together all the bits of evidence that Tom had mentioned. Tom had hinted the robbery would be soon. Just because money was sitting in a bank didn't mean nobody owned it. Quite the contrary, it was the town's source of ready exchange to promote commerce and growth. It included the life savings of hard-working folk. It wasn't right that a bunch of no-good wasters should come along and take it from them.

Chace pulled up about a couple of miles out of Platt's Cut to give the matter some thought. Thinking required coffee and a smoke, so he set to and prepared a small fire while his horse grazed on clumps of vegetation. It's a wonderful thing how a few crushed coffee beans together with some strands of dried tobacco plant can help to settle tricky decisions. For some reason Tom hadn't wanted to enlist the help of the sheriff at Platt's Cut. That was a puzzle. Chace decided the best plan would be to make a well-hidden camp this side of the town. He could ride into Platt's Cut each day, blending with the townsfolk to watch the comings and goings in Main Street and keep an eye on DeSoto's Bank.

By the time he'd found the right spot to pitch camp, ridden into town for a few supplies, got back and cooked and eaten supper, the sky was an all-embracing arch of deep, Prussian blue. Settling down in his soogan under myriad pinprick stars with his horse nearby, Chace's

33

thoughts were suddenly with his friend Tom – God rest his soul. What was it like to be dead? You don't give these things much thought until something happens to make you ponder on the mysteries of life. But before he could fathom an answer, the silent darkness of sleep closed in on him.

As soon as he was awake, Chace threw off the warmth of his night covers and was on his feet. Bringing the fire back to life with some bits of fallen wood, he put his coffee can to boil. Taking a stick of brittlebush from his saddlebag, he peeled back the bark and rubbed his teeth with the cleansing stem. Using the lower branch of a sturdy pine he briskly went through a routine of exercises; he didn't want to lose muscle tone.

Breathing heavily from his exertions, he sat down by the fire as the water began to release its bubbles. He chucked in the pulverized beans and let them stew. He began to think on the task ahead – maybe today would change his life. Maybe tomorrow or next week, or maybe he might lose his life trying to protect a bank and avenge his friend. Whatever happened he would be morally in the right, and that was all that mattered.

He sat a while longer by his early morning fire. It was almost like his days in Lee's army. He dismantled and cleaned all his weaponry, which was now more advanced and more plentiful than in those far-off days – the Winchester, the Colt, a short-barrelled shotgun and the boot pistol. He cleaned and polished his knife with some sand. He saddled the pinto, tightened the cinch and mounted up. Carrying his short-barrelled shotgun across his lap, he set off towards the town with mixed emotions. At the back of his mind was a nagging doubt – what if the

Reeses showed up, raided the bank, and something went wrong? What if one of the customers happened to be handy with a gun and took a chance on plugging the robbers? What if the bank staff included a secret hero who was prepared to take a chance and resist the raid? What if Chace himself got muddled up with the action, was mistaken for a robber and shot? What if?

But that was negative thinking, and he snapped out of it, turning his thoughts to the lure of the North, to forests and lush grass, to herds of beef, a ranch, and one day even a wife ... but that set him off on a completely different track as an image of Roseanne flashed across his mind. Should he have been prepared to stay in the deserts of Arizona to try and win over Roseanne? It was all idle speculation, but it occupied his mind long enough to cover the short ride into Platt's Cut.

Before he rode into town, not wanting to look like a no-good saddle tramp, he dusted off his jacket and shirt, straightened his hat and wiped the dust off his boots. He rode straight up to the saloon with its painted window advertising breakfast. He hitched his horse to the rail and went inside for a good hot meal. After breakfast, he sauntered outside and leant against the railings. Although he appeared somewhat relaxed he was in fact on high alert, his eyes taking in every little detail of the business on Main Street. He noticed a number of men were carrying handguns, no doubt due to the silver prospectors who tended to be highly excitable when registering their claims with the land agent, or lining up to have their rock samples tested at the assayer's office. Mingling with the townsfolk, Chace watched DeSoto's Bank for most of the day. He got a good view of the interior each time people went in and out. At four in the afternoon the bank closed its doors for the day.

Returning to his camp for the night, Chace was beginning to wonder if he should pay the town sheriff a visit and impart what information he had about the likelihood of the Rees gang preparing to rob DeSoto's Bank. Maybe he could just lie in wait for the gang and plug them before they even got into Platt's Cut. But for that he could be charged with murder, unless he could prove they were about to commit a crime. Without any hard evidence, he would have to sit it out and catch them in the act.

After a few of days of keeping a close watch on the town and the people riding in and out, the tension that Chace had felt on the first day had dissipated. This was now just a waiting game, and very boring at that. Time dragged, and the days turned into a slow week – and then, when he was least expecting anything, things happened very quickly.

In the afternoon when there were few customers in the bank and not many people out on the streets, the bank's doors were suddenly closed early. This alerted Chace to what was going on. He rushed to the bank's side window and peered in. There were three men with weapons. It was the Rees gang. They had walked quietly into the bank with total surprise. Heyman had closed the main door and stood on guard, while the brothers got on with the robbery.

'All right, everybody down on the floor. Not you, ma'am,' said Kent, pointing to a young woman in a pretty dress. 'You come here.'

The young woman did as she was bid. Kent grabbed hold of her and used her like a shield. He waved his gun round the room, 'Anybody moves or tries anything, this young lady gets shot. Stay down until we leave.'

The two tellers were awaiting instructions from the manager. All three stood with their hands raised.

A six-gun was levelled at them. 'Put the money on to the counter, notes only, no coins, and be quick.'

The manager took keys from his waistcoat and opened the safe. From his window viewpoint, Chace noticed the manager's eyes darting all over the place looking for a way to stop the robbery. Chace hoped that seeing the hostage, he would have the sense to let the gang take what they wanted and get out. Chace would be waiting for them on the boardwalk and would plug them all as they emerged. If only he could summon help without attracting attention. He needed the sheriff, but there was nobody nearby who could summon assistance, and he was too far off Main Street to shout without the gang hearing him. He had to wait and watch.

'Take these saddle-bags and fill them up,' the young woman was told.

She hesitated.

'Hurry up, you're putting lives in danger.'

She took the bag, approached the counter and filled it with the cash. She seemed to be taking a long time about it and the Reeses were beginning to get jittery.

Bevan was clearly on edge. 'Come on, hurry up!'

As she came back with the saddle-bags, there was a sudden movement behind the grill. One of the tellers pulled a short shotgun from under the counter. Instinctively both the robbers dropped to the floor as the gun was discharged. It filled the room with smoke, noise, flying hot lead pellets and a woman's scream. Before the teller could aim the second barrel, a bullet hit him between his eyes and he crashed backwards, blasting the second load of shot into the ceiling. Clouds of plaster and slivers of wooden debris fell to the floor. The other teller and the manager had taken shelter below the counter.

The customers were still prostrate, hands over their heads to protect themselves from noise, debris and bouncing pellets. The young woman was splayed on the floor, face down, silent, crumpled and motionless. The back of her dress was ripped to shreds, her flesh a bloody mess. She was lying on the saddle-bags. Almost instantly, her body was yanked to one side as Kent grabbed at the blood-spattered bags.

Without further hesitation Chace ran to the front of the bank and blazed a hail of hot lead as soon as the door was opened. Heyman whirled round with the force of a bullet and slumped. In the smoke-filled confusion the Reeses were out of the door and running across the street. Chace fired off three more shots and managed to hit one as they ran across Main Street. Bevan Rees fell to the ground. Kent stopped and returned Chace's fire, shooting wildly with two guns, and scattering townsfolk who were gathering to see what was going on.

The bank manager appeared, covered in plaster and well-shaken. 'Stop them!' he shouted, pointing vaguely into the street. 'We've been robbed!'

It is a strange phenomenon how time can seem to stand still. Crouched in Main Street, reloading his Colt, Chace replayed the last minute in his mind's eye. The sight of the ripped dress, the shattered red flesh, the dishevelled hair. How could he have let that happen? Why hadn't he been able to prevent it? Recklessly and ruthlessly, the gang had caused the death of the young woman and killed one of the tellers.

While all this was flashing through his mind, he was

watching the Reeses trying to make good their escape, Kent dragging Bevan along the ground. One thing Chace had not lost was his calm and methodical manner. Ever since his brief time as a Confederate skirmisher in the dying days of the war, he had known that a cool head and a steady hand are the surest ways out of danger. Suddenly normal time-speed resumed. He fired another shot and Kent sunk down on his knees. Chace rushed across to them.

A crowd now formed a wide circle round the two fallen men with Chace standing over them, the barrel of his Colt still emitting a stream of smoke. Kent was slumped awkwardly and his brother was almost done from loss of blood. Chace's trigger finger was twitching on the gun, mindful of what they had done to Tom. He really wanted to finish them both, there and then. Revenge is a powerful emotion, but vengeance is not the path to justice.

The circle of onlookers was soon broken by the sheriff as he pushed through to see what was going on. He looked at the fallen men, looked at Chace, looked at the smoking gun. 'Hot shootin', Mister. You brought 'em down good. I guess the town owes you a debt of gratitude.'

With a distant look in his eye, Chace simply said, 'There's another one dead in the bank. They're wanted for robbery and murder from here to Texas. I believe a Texas Ranger called Tom Purdy was on their trail. Well, here they are. The law can take its course.'

He had to go through a few formalities with the sheriff and took the opportunity to question the robbers who were in the cell, getting some attention from the doctor. Bevan Rees was hovering on the edge of life, Chace had severed an artery in his leg. Kent was not much better, but at least able to speak.

Chace wanted the last bit of information to complete Tom's work. 'Tom Purdy knew there were two other brothers called Hagen in the gang. Where did they go?'

Kent sneered. 'Find out for yourself.'

'They went to Colorado, didn't they?'

'Did they?'

Chace tried another angle, but later wished he hadn't. 'Did Nickleson kill Tom's wife?'

'Yeah, afterwards.'

'Afterwards?'

Kent sneered again. 'You know what I mean. After he'd gotten the child away from her and sowed his own seed. Killed 'em both with one bullet. He was proud of that.'

Chace wanted to whack Kent Rees for gloating over such a foul deed. Hearing it, he wished he'd been able to make Nickleson suffer a lot more for the scumbag's depravity. It explained why Tom didn't want to talk about Nickleson after Chace shot him. At least Tom had the satisfaction of seeing him plugged.

Chace shook his head at Kent. 'Your life's as good as over anyway. When they string you up, remember Tom Purdy.'

Kent Rees said no more, but clammed up exhausted from blood loss and Chace wasted no more time. He was satisfied the sheriff had enough evidence to ensure they'd both hang for their crimes, including the killing of a Texas Ranger. He didn't want any part of the aftermath, neither the mourning for the young woman, nor the celebration for foiling the bank raid. Chace melted away quietly, unobserved, shunning the limelight. He rode his pinto back to his camp. There were just two images which played over and over again in his mind, both involving people who met a violent end, one deliberately and one accidentally. One whom he knew, and one he didn't. Tom and the young woman. Irrationally, he couldn't stop feeling both of the losses were somehow his fault.

Later that evening, overcome with a delayed weariness, Chace settled his horse with a short-hop hobble and laid out his soogan. He hadn't eaten anything since breakfast. He brewed some coffee, heated some white beans and ate them with some tough corn biscuits. He took the brass star out of his pocket and ran his thumb over its surface to brighten its shine while speaking to it:

'Well, Tom, part of your task is concluded. Those three no-goods have been accounted for. I hate to hear what Nickleson did to you and I now understand what you meant about precious things. I'm not done yet. I'm headed to Colorado to find the Hagens. Ranchers, gambling saloon owners, businessmen, whatever they are now, I'll find them. Wish me luck!'

Exhausted with the day's activity, he decided to turn in for the night. This episode was at an end. He wanted shot of Benton and Platt's Cut. He wanted shot of the hot wastes of Arizona, to erase it all from his mind: robbers, bank raids, bad memories, and even better ones like Rosie, and delivering justice to Nickleson – he wanted an end to the whole lot of it. There was too much sadness adding to what he already had to bear from his past.

Lying in his bedroll, he stared into the grey-black distance with a fixed gaze. The young woman was silently, slowly walking towards him. She looked nervous. Then a shotgun boomed and the scene started over again. He could see quite clearly the deep cream colour of her dress and the little embroidered roses like spatters of fresh red blood. She started walking towards him again and again until sleep released him.

5

Dawn painted its bright yellow streaks into the grey sky, and a new day was beginning. Chace eased himself out of his soogan, yawned, stretched, and began the metamorphosis from sleeping cocoon to waking man. A fire, physical jerks and a roll of tobacco completed the transformation. Before long the water bubbled, the crushed beans brewed, the pinto began to forage, and the sun began to spread a little warmth. Life was looking up. Yesterday he had shunned adulation from the people of Platt's Cut for capturing the outlaws. Justice would take its course, their necks would be stretched, and Tom would be avenged.

Yet today, a cloud of melancholy descended on Chace as his thoughts turned to the young woman. Was she married, did she have children? What about the teller who had fired the shotgun? Courageous, but careless: what he did killed the young woman and cost him his life. Maybe he, too, left a bereaved spouse. Chace still felt partly to blame for their deaths by not intervening sooner.

Doing his best to dispel this sudden melancholy mood, he cleared his camp, mounted his pinto and started the journey north. Crossing a small river of snowmelt rising somewhere far away to the west, he paused and replenished his water bottles. Ahead lay several days of hard riding.

Skirting Platt's Cut, Chace used his spyglass to determine the route. He would need to cross the hills to the north to make his way into Colorado. He sighted some distinctive landscape features to use as waymarkers and fixed firstly on a ranch house a good few miles ahead. Not wanting to revisit Platt's Cut, it would be his best hope for acquiring some food supplies, otherwise he would have to trap whatever he could and start living off the land – no easy matter across sparse, arid wastes.

Coming within sight of the ranch house and seeing a man on a horse, Chace called out: 'Howdy. I'm looking to buy some supplies.'

The man drew his rifle from its scabbard, and cautiously turned his horse. Chace put his hands in the air to show he meant no harm, while not moving his horse at all.

'I don't mean no trouble, mister,' Chace shouted out again. 'Just looking to buy some food. Bread, biscuit or flour and some beans or meat if you have any to spare.'

The man rode towards Chace keeping his gun levelled as he approached. 'You're on my land. Where are you headed, stranger?'

'I'm just riding through,' Chace replied. 'Heading for Colorado.'

'That's a long ride.'

'Way up north, I believe.'

'It sure is. What are you going there for?'

Chace shrugged. 'I'm going to buy a ranch and raise some beef.'

'Keep your hands up high where I can see them,

mister,' the rider continued suspiciously. 'Now if you're here friendly-like you won't mind me looking after your gun while we conduct some business.'

Very slowly Chace lowered his hand towards his holster.

'Stop!' the man shouted. 'Use your left hand and keep that right hand high. Ease the gun out and pass me the butt end.'

With his left hand, Chace removed the Colt and, holding the barrel, held it out.

'All right, move toward me slowly.'

With one hand in the air and the other holding the gun barrel, Chace squeezed his knees and heeled his pinto towards the man, who leaned forwards and took the gun. Getting closer, Chace could see he was in his mid-thirties, well built, with dark hair, blue eyes and a livid scar down his left cheek. The rifle was held firmly under his arm and he managed his horse one-handed with consummate skill. For a moment Chace wondered why he had put himself entirely in this man's power.

'What's your name, mister?'

'Chace. Chace Hexx.'

The man pointed to the scabbard. 'And the rifle, Mr Hexx.'

Chace handed over the Winchester. He didn't feel threatened so wasn't too worried. He hoped to move things along with some friendly chat. Looking at the grazing herd he smiled, nodding his head.

'A fine spread you've got here, mister,' he began, 'how many head?'

'Enough,' was the careful reply. Then, more friendly, 'Are you hungry, Mr Hexx?'

'Sure wouldn't say no to a bite of breakfast,' Chace admitted.

'Come down to the ranch and have some bacon. Ride a little way in front of me and don't mind me being cautious. I haven't been fooled yet by outlaws or confidence tricksters, and I don't intend to start now.'

'That's all right by me,' Chace replied.

Trotting down to the ranch buildings, acutely aware that a rifle was still pointing at his back, Chace's spirits nevertheless rose a good deal. The prospect of some bacon, biscuits and hot coffee was very enticing. As they approached the yard a boy of about eleven or twelve came rushing towards them on a lively pony.

'What you got there, Pa?' he shouted excitedly. 'A prisoner, outlaw, rustler?' He pulled up and looked closely at Chace. 'Is he on the dodge, Pa?'

The man laughed. 'No, Bradley, he's just a fellow out riding. Go and tell your ma to get some coffee and bacon going.'

The boy acknowledged this with a cheery wave, turned his horse and rode away.

'A fine lad,' Chace said.

'The apple of his mother's eye,' the man replied.

Reaching the yard a few moments later, Chace hitched the pinto to a rail and dismounted. The man slid Chace's Winchester into the scabbard on the pinto, but kept the Colt secured in his own gunbelt. Unusually for a rancher Chace noticed that the man's holster was tied round his leg, more often the sign of a gunfighter than a farmer; and the shiny carved walnut butt on his six-gun was evidence of a man who was used to handling it.

The man held out his hand. 'Hardy Elbissen, Mr Hexx. Welcome to my home.'

They shook hands. He pushed open the door and signalled Chace to go in. A delicious aroma of fresh coffee

46

and the sound of sizzling bacon welcomed him.

'Rose, this is Mr Hexx,' Elbissen said to his pretty wife, whose cheeks coloured up as she swept strands of her russet-coloured hair off her forehead and out of her eyes.

'Hello,' Chace said politely. 'Pleased to meet you, ma'am.'

Elbissen turned to the boy. 'Bradley, shake hands with our visitor.'

The boy did as requested. It was clear the man liked things to be done correctly.

'Have a seat, Mr Hexx.'

Chace sat down at the table. Elbissen poured some coffee and pushed the mug towards Chace. How strange that his wife should be called Rose. It sent Chace into a wistful reverie about the Roseanne he'd left behind. Looking around the large comfortable room with nicely panelled walls and furnished not with crudely hewn sticks but with well-made sturdy furniture, Chace imagined himself owning such a place. And then there was the boy, a fine son with good looks and boundless energy rippling in his limbs as he wriggled around on the floor manoeuvring his wooden soldiers in some imaginary battle scene from the war. Yes, that began to figure. Hardy Elbissen must've been a soldier and was now a rancher – but on which side had he fought? It was a dangerous subject to broach and best left alone.

Chace turned his eyes to the cooking range where the pretty young wife was frying up some bacon. This was exactly his kind of dream – a ranch, a son, a pretty wife. When the woman turned to face him asking if he liked his bacon blackened, instead of replying, all he could see was the young woman in the bank walking slowly towards Kent Rees and falling to the ground. He was embarrassingly silent, the words sticking in his throat.

'Mr Hexx,' she repeated. 'Blackened bacon?'

Then, just as suddenly, he snapped out of his reverie with a slight jump. 'Er, yes ma'am, sorry, I was in a daze. Didn't sleep too well last night. I apologize. The bacon'll be just fine, however it comes.'

Having enjoyed a good meal and strong coffee, being allowed to purchase a small pack of food supplies and ascertaining that the next town was some hundred miles away, Chace was ready to leave. Outside, Hardy Elbissen handed him back his Colt and bade him farewell. Bradley asked his pa's permission to ride with Chace to their boundary. They rode off together.

'They were fine little wooden soldiers you were playing with.'

'Yes, my pa made them. He was in the war. He was a colonel in the cavalry. He had a long curved sword and a fine uniform. Two of his men work on our ranch now as cowhands, and we even have a prisoner.'

'You do?'

'Yeah, a man they captured at the end of the war and didn't know what to do with. He said he didn't want to go back to the plantation, so my pa offered him a job.'

Chace reflected on his own situation at the end of the war – although he hadn't been a prisoner he hadn't wanted to go home either, but he had, and then wished that he hadn't.

The boy continued. 'He isn't a prisoner any more, of course. And Pa didn't have the ranch then. They moved out here at the end of the war after the victory over the rebel trash.'

So it was a good thing the war hadn't been mentioned, as Chace and Hardy had evidently fought on opposite sides. And it explained the man's skill on horseback. Now, so many years later, it didn't matter a tinker's damn what colour their uniform had been when two men met hospitably and shared some coffee, so long as the past stayed in its proper place. But the colonel's son already had a lop-sided view of Southerners, and no doubt enjoyed knocking down the wooden Confederates – which is just how these things are perpetuated from one generation to another.

'And you must have been born when it was all over.'

The boy laughed innocently. 'Yes, Pa said I was a "coming home" present for my ma who'd waited so patiently for the war to end. They sold up back east and bought this spread out here. Now we've got workmen, thousands of longhorns and loads of land.' The pleasure was clear to see in the boy's face.

'You must be mighty proud of your pa.'

'Yes sir, I sure am. Maybe there'll be another war and I can be a colonel too!'

After a fifteen-minute ride they came to the ranch entrance gate made up of two big uprights and a curved plank bearing neatly carved words blackened with heat: *Elbissen's Ranch – Bar HE*. There was a fair stretch of fencing on each side of the gate to emphasize that this was private property. It was becoming increasingly common to see stretches of post and wire fence marking off property rights.

'So long, mister,' the boy said. 'Call in when you come this way again and I'll show you my pa's sword.'

Chace smiled. 'Sure thing, sonny. And I expect one day you'll be as fine a horseman as your pa. So long now.'

A hundred miles to the next town meant a steady couple

of days' riding before Chase was likely to come across much in the way of human activity. Hardy Elbissen had told him the main stagecoach track, Aspell Crossing to Platt's Cut, was a couple of valleys over to the east, and that he could easily pick up that trail to make the going easier. Having ridden for a couple of hours Chace thought he must be near the track. But at that moment he heard the unmistakable sound of a gunshot, and when he heard several more, two things were immediately clear – firstly the shooting was just over the next ridge, and secondly it didn't sound like good news. Chace dug his heels into the pinto and quickly ascended the ridge. Reaching the top in double quick time he had a clear view of the road and what was going on.

There were three riders waving guns, one in front of the stagecoach, one behind it, and one dismounting by the door, which was being wrenched open. Four passengers – a man followed by two women and a young boy – stumbled out in quick succession with their hands over their heads. The driver had his hands raised, and the guard was lying motionless, slumped across the seat beside him. The outlaw at the front beckoned the driver to get down, which he did, but as he climbed down he stupidly pulled his gun to take a shot and Chace watched him thrust back by the force of the bullet moments before the sound of the gunshot reached his ears. The driver tumbled to the ground. One of the ladies screamed.

Chace was in a quandary. He was within range with the Winchester, but at that distance a clean shot couldn't be guaranteed. He needed to be closer. But there were three outlaws and only one of him. One good shot could take one of them out, but that would leave two – and what if they decided to shoot the passengers in revenge, or take

50

one as a hostage? Visions of the bank raid flashed across his mind. He couldn't face that scenario again. That would be entirely his fault, and a bad situation would become a whole lot worse. He decided to wait and see what the robbers next move was, robbery being surely their intention rather than murder.

The gang had killed the two stagecoach employees, which meant they were unlikely to hesitate over killing the passengers if they had a mind to. But one thing was for sure: thinking about it wouldn't solve anything, so Chace took the Winchester out of its scabbard, slid off his horse, and using the scrubby vegetation to best advantage, dropped down the slope above the road until he was about a hundred yards off. He could clearly see two of the bandits and all of the passengers, but there was another mounted bandit partly hidden behind the coach. Chace would easily get two shots off before they realized what was happening, and at this range he felt pretty confident of taking out the two robbers that he could see. He raised the Winchester and took aim.

6

Breathing steadily, Chace waited for the best shot. The bandit at the front of the stagecoach climbed on to the driver's seat to retrieve the strongbox. The index finger on Chace's right hand was pressed a little more firmly on the trigger. His heartbeat raised a little and he sensed his best opportunity was about to present itself. There was a chance the bandit with the strongbox would need a hand getting it down. Sure enough, he called to his buddy who came towards the front of the coach.

At the same moment the third robber at the back appeared on his horse, and dismounted beside the passengers. He holstered his gun and searched the male passenger's pockets for cash and valuables. The bandit with the strongbox got his partner to help ease the box off the coach, and he duly took a step up to lend a hand.

It was the exact moment Chace had been hoping for. None of the bandits had a gun in their hand, and all three were concentrating on the act of robbery. It was quite clear the two manoeuvring the strongbox could be taken out quickly. The reaction of the third one at the back was the only thing that worried Chace, but the thought lasted no more than a split second. His mind was made up.

The first shot filled the air with a sharp report and before anyone quite realized what had happened, the second shot also smashed into its target. The two robbers at the front of the coach were thrown back by the bullets – one hung across the driver's seat, while the other one jerked sideways before falling to the ground, but there was still movement in his body and he tried to draw his gun while crawling for cover. Without hesitation Chace put another slug into him and stopped him literally dead in his tracks.

At the back of the coach, the third robber had drawn his handgun, grabbed the boy as a human shield, and was peering in the direction from which he guessed the three shots had come. The other passengers had instinctively fallen to the ground when the shots were fired, the two women trying to shield each other. Chace could see the robber scanning the hillside to try and locate him, but he waited to see what his next move might be. The boy was wriggling, and a good choice for a shield, as he only came up to the man's chest leaving him able to see while keeping most of his body covered. Chace knew that one clean headshot would be all that was required, but with the robber moving his head as he sought out Chace's position, and the boy struggling to break free, it was an impossible target.

The male passenger lying on the ground saw his chance to make a move, and started to wriggle to the side. He was trying to get his hand into his coat pocket without rolling over. Could he be trying to get to a pocket pistol? It was a brave thing if he was. The robber was too intent on keeping the boy in front of him and moving away from the stagecoach to get a better scan of the hillside. He hadn't seen what the man was doing. In the next moment a bullet struck a rock a little to Chace's left. He feared the sun must have glinted on his gun, and given away his position. Then another shot was fired coming close enough to Chace for splinters of rock to be thrown at him.

'Come on out, mister, with your hands up, or I shoot the boy.'

This was the worst of all possible outcomes, the one where everything can go wrong.

The robber continued to shout. 'I'm going to count to five an' if you don't come down the boy gets it.'

There was no alternative. Chace could see the fear and pleading in the boy's eyes. The two women were hoping that Chace wouldn't do anything to endanger the boy. Chace dropped the Winchester and put his hands right up high where the robber could see them.

'All right,' Chace said. 'I'm coming out.'

'You get yourself down here, mister. You shot my two partners so now you can get over here and help me by tying up these people.' His eyes flicked up and down giving Chace close scrutiny – he could see the Colt in its holster, but didn't want to give Chace a chance to use it. 'I can see that gun by your side, so keep your hands up real high.' The robber's gun was now pointing towards Chace rather than being held at the boy's head.

Chace stopped about twenty yards from the robber and stood still. He guessed it was near enough to look willing, and far enough away that the robber couldn't guarantee to hit him with a shot.

The robber laughed. 'Well, you done me one favour I s'pose, at least I don't have to share the loot three ways! Now get over here and give me a hand.'

But Chace knew exactly what was in the robber's mind. It didn't sound unfriendly, he just wanted Chace to go near enough so he could put a bullet in him. Then he would probably kill all the passengers and no witnesses would be left.

So Chace stood his ground.

He was glad he did, for just then providence came to lend him a hand. The male passenger had managed to get his hand to the inside of his coat and pull out the small pistol. Even lying on the ground, at that range he couldn't miss, and as the shot rang out the bandit let out a howl of surprise as the bullet hit him in the arm. Chace had seen what was happening and was waiting for that very fraction of a moment when the robber was thrown off balance. His hand dropped to his holster, pulled out the Colt, and the gun blazed a tongue of fire and smoke. He knew that being quick on the draw was important, but nowhere near as important as being able to shoot straight.

He'd seen many men pull a gun fast, but die because they sacrificed accuracy for speed. In all the years he had been practising with a six-gun the paramount skill had been the ability to shoot five bottles at thirty yards before a count of ten. The skill was in bringing his gun at lightning speed to eye level and shooting off five rounds with pinpoint accuracy. He'd often been asked why he only ever shot five rounds. The answer was simple: six left an empty gun.

Right now he still had five chambers fully loaded and not needed. The robber had been thrown back against the wheel of the stagecoach, with a single, gaping, bloody wound above his right eye as he hung sprawled across the spokes. There was only a twitching movement in his body. The sound of the gunshot had barely cleared as Chace rushed forward to reassure everybody that the danger was over. He checked the pulses on the three bandits and to

55

his surprise there was the faintest of glimmer on the one slumped over the driver's seat.

'This one's still alive,' Chace called out. 'Give me a hand to get him down.'

The male passenger came over and helped Chace lift the man down and lay him on the ground. His life hung on a thread.

'What a mess,' Chace said, as he surveyed the scene.

The two women had got themselves up but were still clinging to each other in a state of nervous exhaustion; it looked to Chace as if they might be mother and daughter.

Chace turned to them. 'It would be useful if he was kept alive even if only to hang him later. A confession to a sheriff kinda ties it up neat. Can you bandage his wound?'

The mother knelt down by the injured bandit and pulled back his shirt to investigate the damage. Her daughter went to the coach in search of some binding rag. The man's shoulder had been smashed, and if he could survive the shock without dying, the wound itself wasn't life-threatening, provided the steady trickle of blood could be staunched.

The boy was sitting on the step of the stagecoach dusting himself down.

'You all right, son?' Chace asked. 'You've had a helluva shock.'

The boy was clearly distraught. His shoulders heaved and tears flowed freely down his face. As soon as Chace spoke to him he wiped them away with his sleeve and defiantly stuck his chin out. 'Grcat shooting, mister!' the boy said. 'I thought he was goin' to shoot you down first.'

'So did I,' Chace. 'So did I.'

Now he had to decide what to do. He couldn't just

leave these people to manage by themselves. He turned to the male passenger and shook him by the hand, saying 'Thanks, mister, it could have been rather different if you hadn't taken that chance.'

'That's what I thought. I prayed to survive when they first attacked the coach, and you must have been the answer to that prayer. But sometimes providence also needs a little help!' He patted his inside coat pocket where he kept the Derringer.

'Can you handle the horses?' Chace asked.

The man looked surprised. In his forties, short and slightly rotund, he was surprised by the request. 'What! And drive the coach?'

'Somebody's got to.'

'I could try, I suppose.'

This was not very encouraging. Chace didn't think the ladies looked as if they would be able to manage the four horses, and he guessed he would have to do it himself.

The boy wandered over, still very upset. 'I could ride a horse, mister, I'm pretty good.'

Chace thought for a moment. 'All right, I need to go and get my own horse. Can you folk gather up these bodies? We'll get this show back on the road as soon as we can.'

Coming back shortly with his own horse and having retrieved his Winchester, Chace organized the party to continue the journey. The boy rode Chace's pinto, leading the other three horses with bodies across their backs, the two bandits on one, the driver and the guard on the others. The women were comfortably seated inside the coach, and the surviving bandit was laid on the floor. Chace took up the driving reins and the male passenger sat beside him wielding the guard's shotgun; he looked the part at least, and had already shown he was ready to act bravely if required. It was highly unlikely that the stage would be attacked twice in the same day, so for the moment everything seemed almost normal.

'Where are you going to take us?' the man asked. 'We were headed for Platt's Cut, is that still possible?'

'Not in daylight,' Chace replied. 'You'd have made it just about, without any delays, but I'm not going to drive this thing in the dark.'

They were silent for a moment while Chace chewed over the options.

'I called in at a ranch this morning, and that might be the best place to head for. I'm sure they would help us out. Maybe we can rest there and start out tomorrow for Platt's Cut. I guess the women need some home comforts and a rest, the boy too.'

'Is it far to the ranch?'

Chace gave it some thought. 'A couple hours, maybe.'

They set off and shortly they came to a fork in the road and an old wooden signpost pointing a finger of wood marked in big black letters: 'HE'.

Chace slowed the horses. 'That'll be the track.' He turned the horses carefully and brought the stage to a halt. Pulling on the break, he jumped down and opened the coach door.

'Are you two ladies all right? I just wanted to let you know there's a ranch at the end of this track and I think we'll be able to stay the night there. Tomorrow I'll drive you on to Platt's Cut.'

The mother smiled at him. 'We truly thank you, mister, from the bottom of our hearts. My daughter Emmie said you were just like the good Samaritan turning up as you did. You could easily have left us to our fate and just kept

58

right out of the way. But you risked your life for us.'

Chace held up his hand. 'Glad to be of assistance, ma'am. Now I just want to get you good folk safely to your destination. We'll be an hour or two now to the ranch, then you can clean up and get some rest.'

He closed the door and turned to the boy riding his pinto, 'You all right, son? Can you ride on for another couple hours?'

'Yes sir, fine and dandy. This is a real smart horse you've got.'

'Well, you take good care of him.' He slapped the pinto's neck, checked that all four corpses were securely tied, then went back to the driver's seat. In a moment they were on their way again.

With a good deal of relief Chace eventually saw the entrance to Hardy Elbissen's ranch. The sturdy wooden gateway was just high enough for the stage to get underneath. He sure hadn't planned on being back here so soon. It was early evening, and three riders with drawn rifles soon came up the track. Chace slowed the horses and brought the stage to a halt. Recognizing that one of the riders was Hardy Elbissen, he stood up and waved his arms in a friendly gesture.

'Mr Elbissen!' he called out. 'It's me, Chace Hexx.' By which time the three riders had reached the stage.

'What exactly is going on here?' Hardy Elbissen asked in his most authoritative voice.

Fortunately it didn't take long to explain the situation and get the whole shooting match down to the ranch, where Mrs Elbissen was waiting at the door. She took charge of the two ladies, while the maid helped the boy down from Chace's pinto. Two ranch hands helped to release the bodies and lay them in a storehouse. The one bandit clinging faintly to life was checked for signs of improvement, but it was determined that to move him might aggravate his injuries, so he was made more comfortable on the floor of the stage.

Later that evening, when everybody had been cleaned up and was recovering from the day's events, they all sat down to a superb stew with corn bread and biscuits. There was beer to drink and coffee at the end of the meal. Gradually as they relaxed the passengers began to talk more freely about their ordeal.

Chace couldn't help his eyes being drawn to the young lady sitting quietly beside her mother. She had beautiful eyes, which she kept mostly downwards, but once she caught Chace looking at her, and immediately her cheeks flushed. Her mother spoke of the life they had just left and their anxiety about making this long journey. She explained that her devoted husband, Emmie's father, who had a textile manufactory, had died in an accident at their mill a few months before. Not wanting to stay amongst so many memories they decided to sell up when they were offered a good price. They were now on their way to California.

'California?' queried Hardy. 'I believe that's a mighty long journey!'

'My sister moved there before the war,' the woman replied. 'Her husband has interests in mining and construction. Emmie and I are going to start a floristry business, aren't we dear?' Emmie looked up and smiled round the table before quickly lowering her eyes again.

Hardy Elbissen, as host, kept the conversation flowing round the table, and he turned to the man who had so far kept fairly quiet.

'And you, sir, Mr. . . .'

'O'Casey,' the man replied, 'Anthony Milord O'Casey – my mother was a hopeless romantic, my initials in Latin spell amo, meaning "I love". She always professed secretly she loved me best, as the first of her nine children. We're of Irish stock you see, came over after the potato famine. I was just ten years of age, too young to remember much about that, except being hungry. But now I'm an American through and through, and am determined never to be hungry again!'

They all laughed as he smiled with his little beady eyes twinkling below a tight crop of prematurely greying hair. And then he turned to Mrs Elbissen and said: 'And if I may say so, ma'am, that was one of the finest stews I have ever tasted, not forgetting we're famous for our stews in Ireland, and I hope it's not too late for me to find a wife who can cook as well as you.'

She acknowledged his praise with a lovely smile. 'So you've come out west to find a wife?'

O'Casey shook his head gently from side to side and shrugged his shoulders. 'Well, not exactly.' He lowered his voice conspiratorially. 'In fact, I'm travelling west to get away from one.'

Mrs Elbissen sucked in a mouthful of air. 'Mr O'Casey, you're a deserter?'

'Oh no, ma'am, quite the reverse, totally the contrary. It was she who deserted me. . . .'

'Because. . . ?' Hardy interjected.

'Because I like to play cards, and when I play cards I like to have a little nip of whiskey. And when I've had a couple of nips . . . well . . . you know . . . sometimes I get lively.'

Chace immediately thought that explained the Derringer in his coat pocket. Mr O'Casey was clearly a gambling man, and judging by the colour of his cheeks, someone who liked more than a couple of little nips. There was even a chance he might have a price on his head, perhaps he had killed someone in a game of cards. But it didn't matter, because the fact was that he had helped save the lives of his fellow passengers, and had provided Chace with the crucial brief moment of opportunity. It suddenly occurred to Chace that nobody knew anything about the boy who occasionally yawned and was sitting next to Elbissen's son, Bradley, with whom he chatted a bit during the meal.

'I think the boy needs to go to bed,' Chace said. 'He's done a grand job riding my horse and leading the others, and he'll have to do the same tomorrow.'

The boy blushed with pride. 'Thanks, mister.'

Elbissen smiled at him. 'Well done, boy! And what's your story, where are you headed?'

The boy gulped down some water. 'Me, sir? My name's Jamie, and I'm headed for California too.' Everyone was silent as if they were waiting for him to explain more. Chace immediately knew he wasn't telling the truth.

'You've also got relatives there?' Elbissen asked.

'Why yes sir, I have, in the mining business. My uncle has a gold mine and he sent us a letter saying he needs more help so I asked my pa if I could go and he said yes, so I decided to go and give him a hand.'

But the more he spoke the more unlikely it seemed, and Chace had noticed the faintest hint of tears gathering in the corner of his eyes. It didn't feel right making him tell lies.

'Well, I need you good and strong for tomorrow,' Chace said, with a reassuring smile. 'So, with Mr Elbissen's permission I think you ought to leave the table, say good-night and get yourself some rest. You've earned it.'

Elbissen nodded. 'That's right boy, you cut along now. Bradley, take Jamie along to your room and get yourselves settled down.'

The two boys left the dining table, and it seemed to be a signal for the party to break up. Mrs Elbissen called the maid, and they started to clear the dishes. Emmie and her mother immediately joined in. The three men retired to Elbissen's oak-panelled study, where he offered them cigars and a glass of whiskey.

'I don't suppose anyone fancies a hand or two of poker?' O'Casey asked.

Both Chace and Hardy laughed.

Undeterred he continued, 'Well, let me show you a trick.' He pulled some playing cards out of his waistcoat pocket. He fanned the cards towards Hardy. 'Now, Mr Elbissen, choose yourself a card.' Elbissen looked suspiciously at the backs of the cards but couldn't see anything amiss so pulled one out. 'Look at your card sir, and commit it to your memory.'

Elbissen looked at the card then, laughing, slid it back randomly into the deck. 'I can tell there is some funny business going on here, O'Casey, but I haven't yet fathomed what it is.'

'Now would you gamble a few dollars if I could tell you what your card was?' Hardy and Chace looked at each other: would they? But before they could answer O'Casey was holding the deck towards Chace. 'And you sir, select one for yourself. Have a look at it, but don't show it to Mr Elbissen.' O'Casey cut the deck. 'Now put it right back in there.'

'And I suppose you could tell me what mine was as well,' Chace said.

'No, sir, I can't . . . but how much would you wager that

it is in Mr Elbissen's pocket?'

'What?' said Hardy, feeling his pocket.

'Surely you'd both be willing to stake something against that!' He took a twenty dollar bill out of his pocket and put it on the desk. 'I invite you to match that with twenty dollars each. But of course you're not going to, however. . .' O'Casey asked Chace to turn round and face the other way, then he fanned the cards face up on to the desk.

Elbissen laughed, 'I might have wagered twenty dollars if you hadn't already told me it was a trick!'

'Quite so,' whispered O'Casey. 'Now Mr Elbissen, pick out the card immediately on top of your own and put it in your pocket.'

Hardy looked down at the deck, he saw his card and on top of it, the ten of diamonds. He picked the card up and put it in his pocket.

'Mr Hexx, please turn round and perhaps you would like to tell us what your card was.'

'Diamonds, number ten.'

O'Casey gestured for him to take the card from Elbissen's pocket.

'Extraordinary!' Hardy and Chace exclaimed together.

O'Casey laughed, 'And I walk out forty dollars to the good. An honest ten minutes work!'

'But how. . . .'

'Gentlemen,' O'Casey began, 'surely you're not going to ask how it's done!'

Elbissen picked up the cards from the desk and examined them closely for any marks or other peculiarities, but could see nothing amiss.

'Tell me tomorrow, Mr O'Casey,' Chace said, 'when I deliver you safely to Platt's Cut.'

'With pleasure, Mr Hexx, with pleasure.'

With that they turned in for the night.

Chace chose to sleep in his soogan on the bench seat in the stagecoach. He said he would be perfectly comfortable, and he wanted to keep an eye on the injured robber.

It was a cold night and the moon was bright. Night insects made their distinctive scraping and chirping noises, an owl hooted, and sagebrush rustled as a nocturnal creature scurried for cover. Chace had put the key to the strongbox in his pocket when he lifted down the driver at the scene. Now inside the coach, he slid it into the lock of the strongbox marked *DeSoto's Bank* in neat, white script. There were letters and documents and four well-filled white linen bags, of the kind that banks sent with bundles of cash and bonds to their various branches. Perhaps these were what the Rees gang were really after. All four of the bags were secured at the neck with lead seals; undoubtedly more than enough to buy a big spread of land and a significant herd of cattle.

Chace sat on the step and rolled a smoke. What a massive temptation. All he had to do was hide the bags in his own baggage, lock the box and toss the key. But he knew he wouldn't do anything of the kind. Like he said to Tom, *I only want to earn my money by honest means.* He drew heavily on his tobacco, causing a bright red glow, then blew the smoke out slowly to curl away into the night. He dropped the end of the cigarette, twisted it into the dirt, got back into the coach, and was soon fast asleep.

7

Chace woke early. The seat in the stagecoach was not the most comfortable place, but he had slept like the proverbial log. The robber on the floor was also stirring and making muffled moaning noises. At least he was still alive, but although his wound had been cleaned and bandaged, unless he got medical attention fairly soon, infection could set in and kill him. It almost seemed harsh to have bound his arms and legs in view of the pain he was in. Perhaps he wasn't worth saving anyway, but then no human life should be described as worthless – not even a bandit's. Chace went into the ranch house, returning shortly with a mug of water. He gently lifted the outlaw's head a fraction, mindful that it would cause him pain in his shoulder, and put the water to the robber's lips, forcing him to sip. The eyelids flickered, but hardly opened – he was hanging on to life by the thinnest of threads. Chace got some more water for a shave.

Before the sun had gone more than thirty degrees into the sky, the stagecoach party, breakfasted and refreshed, was ready to depart. Jamie was riding Chace's pinto and leading the other horses. O'Casey was riding shotgun. Emmie and her mother were seated comfortably inside.

Four dead bodies and one clinging on by a thread completed the entourage. Bradley rode out to the gate with them and waved them off.

'Now, take it easy with the shotgun, O'Casey,' Chace said, looking at him with a serious expression. 'You're a cool shot with a pocket pistol, but have you fired one of these before?'

'No, sir, I can't say I've ever had occasion to fire one of these things. Far too dangerous, in my opinion.'

'Well, I mention it because I expect we might come across a party out looking for the stage. After all, it was supposed to arrive last night and they may be out searching. So if they do turn up, don't go shooting anyone.'

'Indeed not.'

'Unless I say so, of course,' Chace added as a joke.

O'Casey chuckled, and they settled down to the more serious business of getting the stagecoach to Platt's Cut.

It was about an hour after joining the main road that they ran into the search party. Three riders suddenly came round a bend and both parties were as surprised as each other. Belting along at a good speed, Chace had to rein in the horses slowly and it was two or three hundred yards down the road before it came to a halt.

'Stay alert, O'Casey, and keep that shotgun trained on the one who does the talking until I decide whether they're genuine – got it?'

There was no time for O'Casey to reply before the riders appeared at the side of the stage. Doing his best to look the part, O'Casey pointed the shotgun in their general direction.

One of them came to the front as Chace had predicted. He looked up to Chace, 'You've taken your time, we thought you might have broken a wheel or something.

67

You were due in last night. And what's with all these bodies?'

'Are you from the agent's office?' Chace asked.

'Yeah, in Platt's Cut.' He turned to O'Casey. 'And I'd be obliged if you would point that gun somewhere else.'

'Just a precaution,' said Chace. 'They've been held up once already. Three of the bodies are the bandit scum, one of 'em is still clinging on, just. The other two are the stage company men. I'm not the regular driver you know. . . .'

'No, I didn't recognize you,' said the rider.

O'Casey stood up, the shotgun waving about dangerously. 'Now see here, gentlemen, you are in the presence of a genuine hero, a man who risked his own life to save some strangers from a frightful ordeal. Who knows what the robbers intended to do. The two ladies inside, the boy and myself, we owe our lives to this brave man and his skill with a gun. He rescued the coach, and saw us safely to a ranch last night where we were well looked after and had a good night's rest. But now we'd all like to get along to Platt's Cut, so if you don't mind, you can ride ahead and tell them we're on our way. Let's get going.'

O'Casey waved the shotgun in the air somewhat dramatically and, most probably by accident, pulled the trigger. The gun fired a deafening shot into the air, which startled all the horses and propelled O'Casey violently into the seat in a crumpled heap.

Chace steadied the horses with deft jerks on the reins. The three riders of the search party laughed out loud and galloped off towards Platt's Cut. Chace eased the two pairs of horses into a co-ordinated movement, gradually encouraging them into a steady trot, then picking up speed.

'Nice shootin',' Chace said.

'Damn thing's broke my arm!' replied O'Casey, rubbing his elbow, which had crashed against the seatback.

Chace couldn't hide his mirth. 'Well, at least you're now qualified to ride shotgun!'

A couple of hours of steady driving brought the stage to within sight of Platt's Cut nestling amongst the dusty outcrops. Chace realized that despite the hospitality at Elbissen's ranch, yesterday's events must have taken a heavy toll on the four passengers.

'Destination within sight,' he said to O'Casey.

'At last,' O'Casey said, heaving a sigh of relief.

It was after midday when the stage finally arrived in Platt's Cut and pulled up outside the company's office in Main Street. News about some kind of hold-up had reached the town with the three riders, and there was a fair crowd of people gathered around the office. As soon as the stage could be heard rattling into town, the crowd swelled as folk poured out of the shops and saloons to see what all the commotion was about. The company's agent and the sheriff were standing together on the boardwalk.

Chace brought the stage to a standstill and applied the brake. O'Casey jumped down and opened the door for Emmie and her mother, both much relieved to have arrived at their interim destination. Taking charge of the ladies, O'Casey saw them safely across the road to the town's largest hotel and checked them into a room. Meanwhile the luggage was unloaded, and the one surviving bandit was carried across to the jail. The sheriff instructed the doc to try and keep him alive as a suspect, as well as a witness. The undertaker and his young assistant brought a handcart down the street. They carefully lifted in the four bodies which they then wheeled back towards their premises.

Chace helped Jamie off the pinto and congratulated the boy for such a fine display of horsemanship. 'You can take the horses to the livery,' Chace said, giving the lad a significant task.

But Jamie turned away leaving Chace and the horses, and ran up the street after the undertaker. He put his hand on the cart and was soon in deep conversation. Chace watched the lad and wondered. Leaving the stagecoach in the charge of the agent, and giving instructions about taking the horses to the livery, Chace went up the street after Jamie. Arriving at the undertaker's office, he went inside.

'You must be Mr Hexx,' said the undertaker. 'Young Jamie here told me you're quite a hero by all accounts.'

'Never mind that,' Chace replied, waving aside the compliment. 'What is it, Jamie? Do you know these men?'

It was all too much for the lad, and although he tried valiantly to hold back the tears, Chace had just undone the tap and there was no holding it back. He had kept it all to himself, giving nobody any idea why he was one of the passengers on the stagecoach. Even in conversation with Emmie, her ma and Mr O'Casey he hadn't let on who he was. But now there was no holding it back and in a jumble of sobs, tears and blurted words, Chace learned that the stagecoach driver was Jamie's pa. This trip had been intended as a special treat for his thirteenth birthday. His ma hadn't wanted him to go, but his pa had assured her it was safe.

Chace's heart went out to the boy. 'Why didn't you say?'

'I'd already told the other passengers a different reason for me being on the coach. Besides, Pa always said the mark of a true man is how he handles his emotions. I wanted to do him proud.'

Instinctively he put his arm round Jamie and pulled the boy into his chest, letting him release the grief and despair in giant convulsions of his body. It wouldn't be anywhere near enough to mourn his pa, but it would do as a start.

With Jamie by his side, Chace walked back to the company office, where O'Casey was giving an account to the agent. The agent jumped up the moment he saw Chace.

'Please have a seat, Mr Hexx,' he said, offering Chace an open box of cigars. 'I'm Raymond Lewinton, the chief agent for DeSoto Stagecoach Company.' He held out his hand, which Chace shook.

At that moment the office door swung open and a tall, neatly dressed gentleman in a long black frockcoat walked into the office. Mr Lewinton got up from his chair.

'Mr de Soto, come in, sir. May I introduce you to Mr Hexx, the man who saved your stagecoach and the bank's cash sacks. Mr Hexx, this is our worthy bank manager, Harry de Soto, of DeSoto's Bank, owner of the stagecoach company.'

The sheriff chipped in. 'Recognize him, de Soto?'

'Can't say I do.'

'He's the man stopped the bank raid.'

'My goodness, sir! You're mighty welcome. Sorry not to recognize you, I was covered in plaster and bits last time.'

Chace fished in his pocket and pulled out a key which he held out towards de Soto. 'The key to the strongbox,' he said. 'I took it for safe keeping.'

Mr de Soto took the key. 'Thank you. We always make sure the driver has a key to the strongbox. Robbers only tend to kill when they can't get their hands on the money.'

O'Casey interjected, jovially. 'Now then Mr de Soto, I hope the bank is ready to pay a reward to Mr Hexx for saving your strongbox. Platt's Cut has a fine reputation as a prosperous and God-fearing town.' O'Casey was feeling optimistic about innocent prospectors being relieved of a few dollars at a hand or two of poker, or maybe even by the clever deception of a card trick.

De Soto smiled as he opened the strongbox. 'There will, of course, be a reward. The bank would ordinarily pay ten per cent for the return of stolen goods, even in this case when the cash never actually left the stagecoach. It's clear to me you have acted not only very bravely, but also honourably, Mr Hexx. You could easily have removed the contents for yourself. I can tell it's all here, everything I was expecting, and still sealed. Do please call in to my office tomorrow morning. Now gentlemen, I have to get back to the bank.'

O'Casey took Chace and Jamie across the road to the hotel where he had taken the liberty of checking them in for the night. At the reception desk the bespectacled clerk took one look at Jamie and said that they didn't let rooms to young people on their own, he was sorry but that was the hotel's policy.

Just at that moment the sheriff walked into the lobby. 'Hexx! You're becoming a regular hero. First you catch the Rees gang, and now you've saved a stagecoach, what next? Incidentally, one of the brothers you shot, died soon afterwards. The other one'll hang when he comes to trial. People here ain't got no sympathy with robbers. You got any information on a reward for them?' He turned to the desk clerk. 'Now see here, you put this gentlemen up in the best room you got. The town council will pay.'

At that moment the hotel manager emerged from his office. Then seeing O'Casey, 'Mr O'Casey, is this the hero of the hour? Is this Mr Hexx standing next to you?'

The sheriff intervened. 'Yes, indeed. This here is the man who shot the robbers and has now saved the stage-coach. We could do with you here as a deputy, Hexx, what d'you say?'

The hotel manager stepped forward before Chace could answer. 'Let me welcome you to the best and most prestigious hotel in Platt's Cut. When Mr O'Casey came across earlier and checked all five of you good folk into my hotel he told me all about the hold-up and your part in rescuing the de Soto stage and the passengers. I told Jervis to book you the President Suite.'

Chace leaned across to Jervis. 'I guess that has two bed-rooms at least, so the boy can have one of those.'

'Was there a problem?' the manager asked.

'None at all,' Chace said smiling. 'Your clerk was just explaining hotel policy to us, but I think we're all clear about that, aren't we, Jervis? Perhaps Jervis would like to show us to our rooms.'

'We have a boy to do that, Mr Hexx,' the manager said, hitting the desk bell.

Chace immediately muffled the sound with his hand. 'I'm sure you do, but I'd like Jervis to oblige.'

The manager consented and signalled to Jervis to take the keys and escort the guests to the rooms. At the top of the stairs Jervis unlocked the door to the President Suite. Chace took the key and made a point of not giving Jervis a tip, and sent him back to the front desk with a curt, 'Clear off.'

The spacious President Suite comprised two linked

bedrooms and a well appointed sitting room. Chace took Jamie into the smaller bedroom.

'Make yourself, comfortable in here,' he said. 'Then I want us to take a look at the horses.'

A short while later they walked past de Soto's Bank to the livery yard. Chace now had three horses from the bandits which he could claim for himself.

'What'll you do now, Jamie? I guess you better get back home to your ma on the next stagecoach.'

Jamie looked down at his boots and shrugged without any answer.

Chace continued, 'Where is it you're from, anyways? The stagecoach office sign says Platt's Cut to Aspell Crossing, so is that your home or somewhere in between?'

'My home's in Aspell, but it won't be a home no more, not without my pa. I've got one brother and four sisters, and my ma spends all her time with them, making dresses and things.'

'How old is your brother?'

'About two, I guess.'

'He'll need you to be the man of the house, and I reckon your ma will need a strong fella like you to do things round the place.'

'No,' he said desultorily, with a toss of the head. 'She's already got a man for that. Uncle Blake lives local and he's always round. Pa was away a lot, you see, on the stage runs, he didn't only do this route. Ma was always complaining that he was never around when she needed him. Blake used to come round and do all the things she wanted. I didn't like him much and I don't think Pa liked him at all. I guess he'll be round a lot more now Pa's dead.'

There was a long silence. Jamie didn't have anything to

74

add at the moment and Chace didn't want to pursue the subject of this man Blake, as he could see where that might lead the boy. It brought back all the memories of his own mixed emotions when he went home after the war and realized it was no longer the place he wanted it to be. He was about four years older than Jamie then, so how much more difficult this must be for the boy: too young to strike out on his own and too old to be tied to his ma's apron strings. What a difference between this lad's life and Bradley playing with his soldiers, riding his horses, enjoying the freedom of Elbissen's Ranch and a comfortably settled family life.

'We'll think of something. Don't you worry, son. First up we've got to think what to do with all these horses. I can claim six of them.'

They inspected each of the three horses that had belonged to the bandits, and were now by law legitimate bounty belonging to Chace. There were enough witnesses to testify that Chace had saved the stage and was therefore entitled to any bounties and rewards. All three horses were sound in wind and limb, had good teeth and had been well looked after. The saddles were good quality leather with fancy Mexican embossing, and all the fittings were well forged. Two of the saddle holsters had new Spencer rifles and the third a Winchester. It was obvious to Chace that the three men had been professional robbers with plenty of money to throw around. The contents of the saddle-bags added a few interesting items to Chace's booty, including a couple of silver pocket watches, some gold chains, tobacco, and assorted sundries.

'You'll need a horse for yourself, to get to California,' he said to Jamie, whose eyes suddenly widened with interest.

'A horse?'

'Well, I've already got too many and I don't need three more. Which one would you like?'

Jamie immediately went for a fine chestnut horse with its gleaming coat and kind eyes. 'This one, and I'll call it *Diamond* on account of that mark on its forehead.'

'You'd better choose a saddle, and fittings too.'

Jamie looked at the three saddles on the rack. 'I prefer the plain one,' he said, 'it's less likely to get stolen. And do I get the scabbard too, with the rifle?'

'Of course,' Chace replied. 'This is dangerous country with bandits, and who knows what. Can you handle one?'

'I can try. What's yours? Is it a Winchester? Pa said they were the best.'

Chace smiled. 'A Spencer's good too. But I prefer the Winchester.'

'I'll have that one, then,' said Jamie, sliding it out of the scabbard. He ran his hand reverently over the cold metal barrel and the smooth wooden stock.

Just then the sheriff came striding into the yard. He was frowning and had a serious expression. 'Hexx,' he said walking up to Chace, 'I've been lookin' fer you. Come to my office with me, would you? I've got some questions for you.'

8

The sheriff pushed open the door to his office and stepped back for Chace to go in. A deputy was sitting behind the desk, his hat tilted across his face, his boots up on the leather top and a rifle lying casually in his lap. He jumped to his feet as soon as the door opened.

'Take a seat, Mr Hexx,' the sheriff said, indicating an empty chair. Chace sat down and Jamie stood quietly behind him, his hand on the chair back. 'I need to get a full statement from you about exactly what happened to the de Soto stage. I need to know why it was delayed overnight, and precisely when you took charge of the key to the strongbox.'

'I don't like the implication of that.'

The sheriff threw up his hands to deflect any hostility. 'No implication, Mr Hexx, no wrongdoing ain't being suggested, I jes' need to know what happened.'

Chace pointed at the door leading to the cells. 'There's a man in there can tell you what you need to know about the hold-up.'

'The doc doesn't think he'll last the night, lost too much blood.'

'He was the leader of the gang,' Jamie said, coming out

from behind Chace's chair. 'He was the one you should be questioning. If it wasn't for Mr Hexx we'd all be dead and you wouldn't have either the stage or the strongbox.'

'And what exactly were you doing on the stage, son?' the sheriff asked.

Jamie fell silent and retreated behind Chace, his bottom lip trembling.

'All right, Sheriff,' Chace began, 'let me give it you straight.'

For the next ten minutes Chace gave the sheriff all the detail he needed to know – the passengers, the hold-up, the rescue, the overnight stay at Elbissen's, and the day's journey into Platt's Cut. When he'd finished there was a long silence as the sheriff chewed over the facts. Both Chace and Jamie watched his lips rotate as if he were moving a plug of tobacco around his mouth. At last he sucked in noisily, opened his desk drawer, and pulled out some papers and a small stack of Wanted posters. He flipped through them and put two on the desk, which he unfolded and then stabbed with his finger.

'You see Mr Hexx, we've been after these two for quite a while. Looking at the three men you just brought in I'd say the artist has got a good likeness on these two.'

'That's him,' said Jamie, excitedly, 'the one you've got in the cell. And that's the one had his arm round my neck using me as a shield.'

'We think they've been responsible for a number of stage hold-ups across this part of Utah. A federal marshal gave me these posters a couple months back, saying he'd been chasing them all across the territory.'

'And the third man?' Hexx asked.

The sheriff shrugged. 'I don't think anyone had seen

him good enough to give a description, jes' another gang member.'

'Are there more in the gang?'

The sheriff opened his hands, palms upwards, and said 'Who knows? They come and go, some join, some leave. They're drifters. Anyways, you've got yourself a reward for bringing them in. There's a couple thousand dollars on the one dying there in the cell, and four hundred dollars on the one who was holding the boy like a shield. I ain't got no price on the other one yet until the marshal comes by again.'

'Well, when he does, if there's any more money, give it to the family of that young woman shot in the bank raid.'

The sheriff shook his head. 'That's real generous, Mr Hexx. The young woman was due to get married next month, but her fiancé has gone missing, beside himself with grief. Walked off into the desert in his longjohns, carrying a handgun. Don't reckon he'll turn up alive. They were childhood sweethearts an' all. Tragic. That's the side o' things robbers don't ever think about. Anyways, there's still the Rees gang's horses and things in the livery, you can claim all that.'

'I'll just take the horses.'

'Don't s'pose you've considered my offer to be a full-time deputy?'

Chace sucked in sharply. Tom had almost asked the same thing – it was what had started all this off. 'Hell no, you already asked me that. Never fancied being a lawman or a bounty hunter.'

'But you stopped the bank robbery and now the hold-up. . . .'

'Just being a good citizen.'

'Are you planning to stay around a while?'

Chace shrugged, 'A day or two perhaps. I want to see the driver and guard buried decent.'

They shook hands, and Chace and Jamie left the sheriff's office. In their hotel suite Chace took off his boots and jumped on to the bed, stretching himself out with his hands behind his head. Jamie dropped into an easy chair by the window and looked down on the street.

'Well, Jamie, are you going to California with Miss Emmie and her ma? That's what you said. A young man like yourself could do well out there. I guess they'd be only too happy to take you along and look after you for the journey at least.'

'I don't need looking after, Mr Hexx. Not by any more women. California was the first thing that came into my mind. It's where Miss Emmie said.'

'You got a better plan, then?'

'Well, no.' He hesitated. 'Not right now. Where are you going, anyway?'

Chace was surprised. 'Me?'

'You got lots of reward money coming to you and the bank percentage, whatever that means. What you going to do with all that?'

Chace thought for a moment. He wanted to share some plans and ideas with Jamie, but he didn't know why he felt that way. Jamie was a good lad. There was an innocence about him which had taken a severe knock in the last couple of days. He was on the cusp of a disappearing childhood and the advent of adult responsibilities. The lad needed to make a decision about his suddenly uncertain future.

Apart from Tom, Chace had never really shared any plans with anybody. He hadn't really even told Roseanne very much before asking her to go with him. He was too much of a loner. Tom's death made him even more reluctant to talk to anyone about his hopes for the future. So why burden a young lad with his dream: was he really a loner, or just lonely?

'You could buy a ranch and raise horses with all that money,' Jamie observed while still looking out of the window.

'Is that what you'd do?'

'It's what my pa said he'd do when he finished with DeSoto, if he had enough money.'

'You like horses?'

'Got one of my own back in Aspell. I ought to go back there and get her, but I don't want to see any of my family in case I change my mind about leaving. It's more difficult when people start talking at you and trying to keep you back.'

'Would that happen?'

'I guess it might. I'm fond of some of my sisters and they like me too, not all of them. But you know ... I wanted to work with my pa raising horses.' Jamie's voice trailed off with a slight quiver and Chace didn't want to press the subject.

'Well, why don't you have all my bounty horses – I sure as hell don't need them. There's six now, you'd have seven adding your own horse from Aspell.'

Jamie swung round, his eyes bright with enthusiasm but glistening with the hint of those tears that he wanted to weep, but wouldn't. 'You mean that?'

'Sure,' said Chace. 'I might even buy you a ranch to put them on!' He wasn't sure why he said that, but it was too late to retract. He couldn't say something like that and then shatter the boy's dream so quickly. 'You asked me what I was going to do – well, I'll tell you. I was making my way up north, Wyoming or Montana, where I plan to buy some land. I'd been at Elbissen's ranch when I luckily came across the de Soto stage hold-up – and you know the rest.' He didn't mention the unfinished business of hunting down the Hagen brothers from Texas.

'So I could come with you? Is that what you're saying?'

Chace looked long and hard at Jamie, narrowing his eyes and looking for all the possibilities he might see with his mind's eye. He could certainly use some help on a ranch, though he'd never thought of having such a young lad to help him. On the other hand, if he was truly going to raise some beef, having responsibility for Jamie would certainly keep him focused. If things didn't work out, well, that was in the lap of the gods. It doesn't do any good to look too far ahead with hopeful human eyes. The future has a way of messing things up.

Chace nodded. 'Yeah, I guess so. We'll need to kit you out with a few things for sleeping rough and some personal equipment. It's a long ride – weeks and months, not days. What d'you say?'

'And the ranch?'

'I'm going to raise beeves, but you can do horses if you want – but you got to do something with them.'

'That's a deal, Mr Hexx.'

There was no more discussion about this plan. In fact even when Chace, Jamie, Anthony O'Casey, Miss Emmie and her ma were having dinner together that evening, neither Chace nor Jamie said anything about it.

Making polite conversation, Emmie turned to Jamie. 'Do you want to travel with us to meet your uncle in California?'

Jamie was equivocal. 'That's very kind, but I haven't yet decided on the next bit of my journey.'

After dinner Chace and Jamie went across to the sheriff's office to see about the reward money. The sheriff said to call in and see de Soto the following day around mid-morning and the money would be waiting for him. Jamie wanted to go and have another look at the horses, so they walked along to the livery yard.

'We'll have to go north via Aspell Crossing to collect your own horse.'

Jamie looked away. 'You can collect it for me.'

There was no point pursuing the subject. 'We'll decide when we get there.'

They spent a while checking over the horses, then went back to the hotel's saloon bar and sat at a table. Chace had a beer and rolled himself a smoke. Jamie watched O'Casey playing poker with some men. It didn't look as if he was doing too good, his stack of money seemed to be going down rather quickly. Jamie whispered to Chace that O'Casey was losing a lot of dollars.

Chace leant across to Jamie and whispered back, 'Don't you worry about Mr O'Casey, Jamie. Just keep an eye on him and learn why you shouldn't play poker with someone you don't know.'

Miss Emmie and her ma came into the saloon. Chace stood up and greeted them warmly. 'Ladies, please join us.' He pulled back a chair for Emmie's ma, and she sat down. Emmie took a seat next to Jamie. Jamie kept flicking his eyes across to O'Casey, and was amazed to see the stack of bills and coins starting to grow. At the same time he was listening to Chace chatting with Emmie's ma about their California venture. Chace still didn't let on that he was going to take Jamie as a ranch hand. A tray of tea arrived for the ladies, and O'Casey's cash pile had shrunk again, this time to almost nothing. Emmie started to ask

Jamie about his uncle's gold mine. Thankfully, Chace saved him by diverting Emmie's attention. Jamie turned back to O'Casey and noticed his pile of dollars had suddenly grown into several stacks and voices were being raised.

'Put your hands on the table!'

There was a sudden commotion as chairs were pushed back. Two of the players got up and moved quickly out of the way, and onlookers began to move aside. O'Casey sat quite still with his hands spread palm downwards on the table. Opposite him, the third man who had been playing poker at the table was standing, a six-gun in his hand pointing at O'Casey.

Chace leant across to Jamie. 'Slip out the back quickly and get the sheriff.'

The gunman was beside himself with rage. 'Now you tell me how you got four of a kind without cheating, mister.'

'No cheating, I assure you,' O'Casey replied calmly.

'You're a liar. You were near busted out, now look at that stash, you done that by cheating an' I ain't seen no four of a kind for a long whiles.'

'But you dealt the hand yourself,' O'Casey protested. 'How could I have cheated?'

'I dunno, you tell me.' The man drew a long-bladed knife from inside his coat. 'Now loosen your tongue, I'm going to cut off your little finger if you don't tell me how you done it.'

The air was very still in the saloon; the tension could be felt almost throbbing through the furniture, and tobacco smoke was rising upwards in straight lines instead of being blown out in fragrant clouds. Conversations had stopped mid-sentence, and virtually all eyes were turned towards the poker table. The man started to move round the table, his gun still pointing at O'Casey's head.

The barman put down a glass noisily on the counter. 'Porky! There ain't no need fer that. If you dealt the hand, you're responsible.'

' 'Sponsible! F'losing my money? No, this fella's been cheating several hands now.'

The room was so quiet the hammer cocking and chamber engagement on Chace's Colt was almost deafening in its deliberate and slow metallic menace. 'Take another step, Porky, and your brains will decorate the ceiling,' Chace threatened calmly.

Porky stopped still, but didn't turn round to see exactly who had spoken to him – but nor did he lower his gun.

'Well, fella,' Porky said to O'Casey, 'looks like you've got a friend in here.'

Chace stood up very slowly, crossed the room, and moved to within a few yards of the poker table, his Colt held very steady at arm's length and head height. 'Lower your gun real slow or this ends in one of two ways, Porky, with you dead, or with you dead. Choose now.'

Appearing quietly from the hotel lobby the sheriff came into the saloon, Jamie hovering in the shadows behind him.

'Well, Porky, what you done this time?' the sheriff asked. 'Now put that gun away and hide your knife. If you can't stand losing, you shouldn't be at the table.'

It was a well considered intervention. There was no threat to Porky from the sheriff, he simply used his authority to calm the tension. 'It looks to me like you've upset Mr Hexx, and made us look like inhospitable folk. I guess Mr O'Casey jes' wanted a quiet game of cards.'

'I'm no cheat, sir,' said O'Casey to Porky, visibly

relieved that the temperature had dropped a few degrees. 'I do agree with you that four of a kind doesn't come up often in one hand, and since you dealt the hand, I'll even give you some of your money back as a sign of goodwill.'

The sheriff smiled. 'You can't say fairer than that, Porky.'

The incident was over, conversation started up at once, and the barkeep pulled beer to wet the throats of the townsfolk dried up with tension.

Chace lowered the hammer and slid the Colt back into its holster. Sitting down again at the table, Emmie's ma said that was the second time he'd saved O'Casey. Chace laughed. He congratulated Jamie on managing to bring the sheriff across through the hotel rather than crashing through the batwings, which might have caused gunplay. The poker game resumed, but without O'Casey who came across to his fellow passengers. He proposed to stand a round of drinks.

'I sure ain't goin' to be behind you all the time, O'Casey,' Chace joked.

'I lead a charmed life, Mr Hexx. There's no need to worry on my account.'

He walked across to the bar to buy the drinks. Chace shook his head and laughed, but as O'Casey walked past the poker table, Chace caught Porky's eyes narrowing to focus on O'Casey's back. Goodwill probably hadn't been restored, despite the generous return of some of Porky's dollars. Chace studied Porky's sly features: he had an air of hostility and an aura of trouble. It might be best to keep well out of his way. In any case he and Jamie would be leaving Platt's Cut tomorrow. O'Casey would have to fend for himself.

At the end of a convivial evening the ladies retired to

their room. Jamie went to bed, and Chace invited himself into O'Casey's room for a nightcap.

'Men like Porky are dangerous,' Chace said.

'Oh, I know that. I make my living out of cards, Mr Hexx. It tends to upset a lot of people, which is why I keep moving on. Anyway, Porky is lucky to be alive. I would have shown him how I cheated by indicating the inside pocket of my jacket. He would have let me explain, people like that are always too curious for their own good. Revealing the secret pocket I would have moved very slowly and carefully, then suddenly shot him in the head with the Derringer. He would have joined a long list of foolish gamblers.'

'So you did cheat?'

'No, I don't need to cheat. I play the odds, I know about cards, I understand the game. Four of a kind was a touch lucky, I admit that. I hardly look at the cards. I'm a professional, Mr Hexx, and a good one. Amateurs keep looking at their cards, pros look at the other players, that's how you know when to bet and how much to wager.'

'But you did cheat with that card trick out at Elbissen's.'

'Not exactly. I'll show you how.' He took a deck of cards out of his jacket pocket. 'I always carry these on my person. I would have used them tonight in the unlikely event of me losing at poker.' He handed the deck to Chace. 'You can inspect the cards if you wish.'

'Waste of time,' said Chace, 'if there's anything crooked about the deck I sure ain't goin' to spot it.'

'Wise man, Mr Hexx, wise man.' O'Casey fanned the cards, 'Take one. Now, while you look at your card, yes look at it, I'm going to turn the deck round in my hand. Now, slide your card back in anywhere you like.' He handed the deck to Chace. 'Feel down the side of the deck, one card is just very slightly sticking out, yes?'

'Yes it is, I can just feel it. My card I suppose.'

'Of course. It's a tapered deck you see.'

'Tapered?'

'A magician's deck. The cards are not exactly rectangular. The deck is fractionally skimmed obliquely down one side. If you take a card out, and the deck is turned round, when you slide it back in, it sticks out minutely at the side. As for the rest, I can't give away too much but you see the general idea?'

'I always thought gunplay was a dangerous game, but I guess it's actually a lot safer than yours! Now listen, I reckon Porky is looking for trouble, so make sure you lock your door, bar the window and sleep with a gun nearby. Good night now.'

'Good night, Mr Hexx, and thanks.'

It was the last time they spoke. When Chace went down with Jamie in the morning he wasn't surprised to learn that O'Casey had already checked out and left. Perhaps Platt's Cut had already proved too hot for him.

They breakfasted with Miss Emmie and her ma. Chace told them he would be leaving town and heading north later that day, after the funerals for the stagecoach driver and the guard. Jamie said he had decided not to go to California after all and was going to ride north with Chace. And so the episode ended, and the ad hoc party thrown together by a stagecoach hold-up dispersed.

Chace and Jamie mounted up at the livery. By the time Chace had collected the reward money from the sheriff and the payout from the bank, he was leaving Platt's Cut with more money than he'd ever dreamed of. He turned to Jamie. 'Well, Jamie, this is where your new life begins.

Mine too, I guess.'

Jamie gave him a brief smile, but the emotion of the funeral was still visible on his face.

By the time they were fully kitted out for their long journey it was late afternoon. Chace was riding his pinto, and Jamie thrilled to be on Diamond, his gleaming chestnut, with five more good horses in tow. He was beginning to feel he was crossing the threshold into adulthood, not least because he had a Winchester in the saddle scabbard, a brand new Schofield .44 revolver on a gunbelt, and the guidance of a man who could show him how to use them both. He could hardly wait to get some practice. Little did he know that there wouldn't be time for any practice before he would be trying to shoot for real.

9

With the sun on its descent, Chace was impatient to leave the place and get on with his journey. After all, he'd only come back to Platt's Cut on account of delivering the stage back to the DeSoto company. Now he'd taken on another responsibility, a young lad mourning his pa, not wanting to go back to his home. He knew exactly how the kid must be feeling, and he knew, too, that the best cure would be a clear vision of an exciting future. For that reason, Chace thought it best to get on the road. He took one of the horses for his gear and Jamie led the others.

They had ridden about an hour, maybe more, when Chace was suddenly aware that they were not alone. His sixth sense was itching and his hackles were up. He had the distinct feeling that eyes were on them. The ridge to the left of the track would afford enough cover for a stalker, and with the sun sinking behind the ridge, it would be difficult to see an outline against the strong rays of the sun. If they were being tracked, perhaps whoever it was would hold off until they pitched camp for the night and strike in the dark. Chace couldn't take that risk.

'Jamie, don't look at me or anything, just keep riding as if I wasn't talking to you, but listen carefully and do exactly what I say. We have company, an' that company isn't good news. They've been stalking us since we rode out. I want you to ride on a bit, slow to start with, then quicken up and break away. You'll hear a shot but don't worry about that. Once you get round that bend, get off the track into the brush. Tether the horses and double back here. Stay low and watch good. I've got to sort this out before it gets too dangerous. Now move off.'

Without looking at Chace, in fact playing the part well, Jamie heeled his horse into a slightly quicker pace, and dust began to rise from all the hoofs. Chace had slowed, and it looked as if he was just dawdling along without a care in the world. Then Jamie gathered speed.

'Hey! Hey, boy!' Chace called, almost standing in the stirrups. 'Well, I be doggone,' he said, sliding the Winchester out of the scabbard. He levelled it as if taking aim and fired off one round. Then sitting back down, he sheathed the rifle and jumped down off the pinto, pretending to check the cinch. He was hoping that anyone intent on ambushing him might be drawn out into the open. Most of Platt's Cut would know about the large sum of reward money he was carrying. Chace's senses had been on high alert for an attempt at robbery. Killing him and Jamie outright might be someone's plan, and being shot down, especially as he was now on his own, was a calculated risk. But Chace was sure these weren't professional outlaws, or he wouldn't have detected them. He gambled on them being chancers who were more likely to engage in bragging conversation. He guessed one in particular was out for revenge. They would be full of bravado, enjoying the thrill of having the upper hand – and that would be their undoing.

Chace remounted, but before he could move off, two

riders appeared. One came down the ridge in front on his left side and his partner pulled up behind Chace out of sight, stopping close enough for Chace to hear the jingle of the chain and bit, as the horse tossed its head.

'You ain't quite so smart now. Keep your hands up real high where I can see 'em.'

Chace put his hands up. 'Damnation. It looks as if the lad has just stolen all my horses and ridden off. And I guess your boss is still sore about the poker game and he's hoping to get some money back by stealing from me. It's not my day, is it?'

'I ain't working for no boss,' the man said getting off his horse and coming across to take Chace's Colt. He chucked it on the ground without emptying the chambers, confirming he was no professional robber. 'It won't have escaped your notice you've got a gun trained on your back, so don't do nuthin' silly. Where's the money?'

'It's on my other horse,' said Chace, indicating the one behind him. 'The leather bag attached behind the saddle.'

'This one?'

Chace looked round. 'Yeah, that one.'

The robber undid the buckles. 'It's empty, you lying . . .'

'What!' Chace exclaimed. 'That dirty, double-crossing little sonofabitch. That's why he's gone off so fast. Well, that's it. Unless you catch him there ain't no money to speak of for anyone, except the boy. He'll be long gone by now. Can I just have a look myself at the bag? I can't believe this, there was more than ten thousand dollars reward money in there.'

This sudden turn of events caused both the would-be robbers to lower their guard just a little. It put them off the main business of carrying out the robbery, and changed the tone of the situation. Chace had diverted their attention away from himself on to the disappearance of the boy, and it suddenly looked as if the robbery had failed. Neither of the guns were now pointing directly at him.

'Well, go right ahead. Look for yourself, mister, and keep those hands up high. The bag's empty.'

Chace casually slipped down off his horse but there was nothing casual about the way his eyes were working. The masked gunman on horseback was the greatest danger. Chace knew it was Porky. Chace's hands were high but there was one place on his way back to his pack horse where the rider's line of sight would be interrupted. It was no more than two feet of opportunity and Chace's muscles were tightening for action.

Suddenly crouching down Chace's left hand scooped a handful of dirt which he threw into the face of the man standing by the empty saddle-bag, while with his right hand he pulled a small pistol from his boot and blasted a shot at the horseman, knocking him clean out of the saddle, a patch of deep red blood spreading across his shirt. By the time the other gunman had recovered from the shock of the attack, with dirt still in his eyes, Chace had laid him out with one massive punch to the jaw which connected with a nasty cracking sound. Chace dragged him to the side of the road, then pulled the mask off his shattered accomplice and realized too late it wasn't Porky. He went to pick up his Colt. As he bent down there was the crack of a rifle shot, the bullet thudding into the ground barely a foot away, spitting dirt into his face. Chace scooped up the revolver and took shelter beside the horse's flank, giving this new assailant nothing to shoot at.

'Well now, thinkin' you'd won, didn't you?' came the distant gloat.

Chace didn't have to see the man to know who it was. He cursed himself for his carelessness. He should've scanned the ridge by eyesight. He knew he could smell more trouble, and yet he'd let Porky get the upper hand. It was so careless. But the glimmer of hope was that Porky would be another talker, another chancer playing at being a bandit.

'All right, Porky,' Chace shouted, while remaining well hidden behind the horse's side. 'What is it you want?'

'You know what I want, mister, git out with yer hands up or I'll plug the horse until I get a clear shot at you.'

'Whoa!' Chace shouted back. 'There ain't no need to shoot the horse. I'll come out if you agree not to shoot while we discuss this, and then let me get on my way. The money's gone, anyway.'

'Like I said, mister, git out with yer hands up high or the horse gets peppered.'

The longer Chace could keep him talking the more likely Porky would lose concentration. Greenhorns like the sound of their own voices when they think they're calling the shots. Unfortunately for Porky it wasn't him calling all the shots right now. Though Porky didn't know it, and neither did Chace, not more than fifty yards away in the scrub, the barrel of a Winchester rifle was being carefully lined up on Porky's chest.

Chace was eager to keep buying time. 'Look here Porky, I just told your two friends the money ain't here. The boy has stolen it and ridden off. The longer I'm kept here, the less the chance there is of me catching him and getting it back. I earned that reward money fair and square. Let's do a deal. You can have half the money if you ride with me and catch the boy. How's that sound to you?'

Porky burst out laughing, but the mirth was cut short by the loud report of a rifle shot. Chace immediately thought Porky had shot off a round at his pinto. He wasn't going to stand for that, so he threw himself down on the ground into a roll under the horse, and fired off a wild shot in Porky's direction. Porky had ducked to the side and now swung himself back into an upright position and Chace could see him taking aim with his rifle. The position of Porky's horse prevented Chace from getting a clear line of sight on Porky's forehead or chest; he wavered. All of this took no more than a few seconds of sheer panic. Then Chace heard a second shot and braced himself for the inevitable impact as he dropped flat to the ground. But he felt nothing and waited for the sensation of trickling blood.

'That was a close thing!' Jamie said, as he came up to Chace. 'I guess I missed him with the first shot, this gun's got a helluva kick, but I got him real good with the second one. Maybe the sight on this gun needs adjusting.'

For a moment Chace lay completely flat on the ground. Then he started laughing. At first just a gentle snorting, then soon they were both heaving with convulsions at Jamie's wise observation. Eventually dusting himself off, Chace looked at Jamie shaking his head. 'I thought you'd forgotten to come back. And how did you manage to stay hidden like that?'

'I saw him on the ridge, that Porky, the one I've just shot. But I couldn't warn you while you were dealing with the other two.'

Chace nodded. 'You're one hell of a lad, Jamie. Your pa would be real proud of you, and so am I. And you know what, you've just got yourself three more horses.'

Jamie's bottom lip trembled at the thought of his pa buried in Platt's Cut, and a tear formed in the corner of his eye. He wiped it away and turned to Chace. 'All we need now is some cattle for you.'

'I can wait,' said Chace. 'Now you see why I had that extra horse. I knew Porky would want revenge.'

'You thought it all out real good.'

Chace shrugged. 'Remember two things, Jamie. Expect the unexpected, and in the last resort, don't sacrifice accuracy for speed. That way you get to stay alive.'

They put the two dead bodies beside the road, tied the hands of the one Chace had knocked unconscious, removed all their weaponry, strung the horses into a line, and rode off.

'Shouldn't we have done something for the injured one, Mr Hexx? He might die of cold overnight, or be attacked by wolves.'

'Listen, Jamie, you only show compassion to those who deserve it. Any one of those three would have killed both you and me without a second thought. I've left him with a chance to live, some would have hung him or shot him in cold blood, and it would be what he deserved. Look after yourself and your buddies, an' don't trust nobody else. Clear?'

'Clear.'

The last glimmer of daylight was disappearing from the sky as they sat by the blazing fire waiting for the beans to soften. Chace had brewed some coffee, and although Jamie found it rather bitter, he knew he was going to have to get used to it in the coming days.

That night as he lay awake looking again at myriad pinpoints of white light in the infinite darkness, Chace felt, for the first time, that his life really had begun to turn round. It was strange how things were happening. It was purely by chance that Tom had found him working at the livery in Benton, and called on him for help in catching the Rees gang. That all went wrong for Tom. Then the events at the bank raid in Platt's Cut to avenge Tom, which had also gone disastrously wrong, more lives having been lost before he plugged the outlaws.

Since then he had killed three bandits and saved four passengers, one of whom was asleep by the fire. Then they'd put a stop to volatile Porky and his associates. It was a crazy world of checks and balances. Yet out of it all he had lawfully earned enough reward money to get started raising beef, and overall if there really was a day of judgement to be faced when you died, maybe the scales were tilting. His good deeds might just count in his favour, and the thought lulled him into a righteous sleep.

After a couple of days' riding they were within reach of Aspell Crossing. Chace agreed to go to Jamie's house with the news of his pa's death and to collect his horse. He understood why it would be difficult for the lad to deliver that message and then just walk out. Aspell was a busy town, and Jamie didn't want to go anywhere near it in case he met anyone he knew. When they came within sight they took a wide detour and found a suitable place to pitch camp. Chace left Jamie with the horses hobbled and grazing, and rode down into town. Following precise directions he found his way to the plot of land and two-storey wooden house where Jamie's ma and family lived. It was mid-afternoon and the sun was still giving out lots of heat. Chace pulled up at the gate, dismounted and hitched the reins to a fencepost.

A dog came up to the fence barking and wagging its tail, followed closely by a small boy who tripped and fell in his rush to see the stranger. The dog immediately ran to the fallen toddler and started bouncing round and licking his head. The commotion brought a woman out of the house into the front patch. She was slender, rosy-faced and smiling, her hair gathered in a loose chignon. She was wearing a long checked dress with a white apron, and as she approached the gate, brushed away wisps of hair with the back of her hand. A young girl came running out at the same time, picked up the toddler and set him on his feet.

'Ma'am,' Chace said, taking off his hat. 'Are you Jamie's ma?'

The next hour was the most difficult Chace had passed since the siege at Petersburg, and far more distressing. He sat with them while they wept, tried to answer their questions. He found it very difficult to say that Jamie had decided to move on and seek adventure further west. Jamie had insisted that Chace should say he had gone to California, but in front of his ma and his sisters he found the words kept sticking in his throat.

It had been difficult, too, to lie about the horse. Jamie told him to say that he wanted Chace to have his horse as a gift for saving his life in the robbery, but untruths seemed harder to utter in the face of the family's distress. Covering other people's lies made him feel uneasy. But right now his duty was to Jamie, and he did exactly as Jamie had requested.

Before leaving, he handed over the widow's payment from the DeSoto Stage Company, given to Jamie to take back to his ma. It wasn't much, but would likely be enough to live on for a while. Jamie's ma was an attractive woman, and the chances were she would remarry, maybe the man called Blake whom Jamie disliked.

Taking his leave, it broke his heart to see the girls with their red eyes, and the toddler confused by the whole affair. Jamie's ma had composed herself, but when she thanked him and gave him a warm hug for bringing the news and the money, it was Chace who began to feel a pricking in his eyes. He turned away quickly, mounted up and with Jamie's horse attached behind by a leading rein, waved his hand and rode off.

Riding down Aspell's broad street, he managed to keep everything in check, but as soon as he left the town's last buildings the tears began to flow down his cheeks, and irregular gasps choked his breathing. He felt ridiculous, blubbing like an infant, and rubbed at his eyes with the back of his sleeve – but it suddenly dawned on him that this was the long-buried parting from his own family. Just like Jamie, he had left without seeing them, had left without the conclusion of a goodbye, a proper leave-taking. It was the closure that never happened, leaving a deep-down wound that would one day burst open. Today, that day had come for Chace, and one day in the future the same would happen to Jamie.

Chace rode out to the camp with mixed emotions. On the one hand there was a sense of relief that everything associated with Platt's Cut had come to an end. But at the same time he was concerned that maybe he wasn't doing the right thing by Jamie. Even if the lad didn't want to go home, it wasn't Chace's prerogative to actively encourage him to leave his family. Somehow, without the slightest intention of doing so, he had effectively enticed him away, giving Jamie the horses and an implicit share in a ranch. It was easy to see why the boy was happy to throw in his lot with Chace. And thinking of favours, Jamie had already returned the life-saving favour by shooting Porky at the crucial moment.

Chace concluded, as he always did, that you have to look after yourself in the first place and let others do the same, let them make their own decisions. As soon as Chace came within fifty yards of the camp, Jamie ran out of the cover to greet his horse, throwing his arms round its neck. The horse responded with a cheery snort, tossing its head.

'Gee, thanks Chace, she means so much to me, being a present from my pa an' all.'

They sat down together by the fire later that evening waiting for the bacon and beans to cook and the twists of corn dough to turn into bread. Jamie was drinking water as he hadn't yet got used to the bitterness of the coffee. Chace was pulling on one of his hand-rolled smokes. In the stillness, they could hear the crackling of the fire punctuated by the mournful wailing of a screech owl. A high-pitched yowl suggested there were kit foxes with cubs in the neighbourhood. Moths danced into the fire-light and a spotted bat soon latched on to an easy meal.

The two humans were far away in their own thoughts. They would have liked to have known what the other was thinking, but they didn't encroach on each other. Chace was surprised that Jamie never once asked after his ma or his siblings, and Jamie was equally surprised that Chace never mentioned them. As the temperature began to drop they were glad of the fire and the sanctuary of their soogans. Both were privately conscious that a chapter of their lives was closing, and a new one was about to open.

10

So began their long trek out of Utah and into north-west Colorado. After just a few days in the saddle, Jamie wanted the riding to come to an end so he could start looking after his horses properly. He liked the look of Colorado, but Chace kept moving from town to town, some no bigger than an outpost. Everywhere they went Chace disappeared into every saloon he could find. Jamie began to think something was up, maybe he was getting a drinking problem; Chace would never say what he was doing. At least they were riding through better vegetation and Jamie wasn't having to worry so much about finding forage for the horses.

As they passed through small townships Chace stocked up on bacon, flour, beans, jerky, coffee, biscuits, cheese and tobacco. They bought extra horse feed from corn merchants. They filled water bottles from rivers and streams. They slept underneath the stars and occasionally put up at a hotel, and rested and groomed the horses at a livery. Every now and then, Chace would make use of the barber shops to take a bath and have his beard shaved.

'Mr Hexx,' Jamie began one day, with all the politeness

he could muster, 'you seem to be drinking a lot these days.'

Chace looked at the boy, mystified. Then he cottoned on and laughed out loud. 'Ha! Ha! Yes, you're right. I've got the very devil of a thirst. But not for whiskey. You're wondering why I keep going into the saloons.'

'Well, yes sir, I am.'

Chace hadn't yet told Jamie about Tom Purdy or the Hagens. But now he decided it was time to let the boy know why they'd have to stop temporarily in Colorado instead of riding on into Wyoming or Montana to look for land. They stayed that night in a ramshackle building unreasonably calling itself a hotel. Over a tough and taste-less steak, Chace told Jamie the full story.

When Chace had finished, Jamie had a resigned tone to his voice. 'I guess that's unfinished business,' the lad said with a shrug of the shoulders. 'And have you got a lead on the Hagens yet?'

'A possible lead. Someone told me there were people living near Black Creek by the name of Dagen or some such. Big ranch owners. Could be just a simple name change, Hagen to Dagen. You see, Jamie, I couldn't start afresh until the score is settled and Tom fully avenged. What that gang did to him was unspeakable and it's not right that they should profit by robbing hard-working, honest folk; killing and raping with total disregard for the distress they leave behind. Tom Purdy was a Texas Ranger, and he paid with his life for trying to bring them to justice.'

'What makes you think the same won't happen to you?'

Chace shrugged. 'It might. Of course it might, but you have to do what you think is right. Better to die for what is right than to turn a blind eye and hope somebody else will step in for you.'

'Will you kill them if you find them?'

'That's not my job. All I want to do is what's right, and let the law decide the rest. Tom was a decent man with a family, and everything was ruined by that gang.'

No more was said on the subject.

Moving on the next day, the land was deeply ravined with red earth cuts, fringed with pine forests. Flat-topped buttes with sheer sides rose into the sky. Valleys were watered by well-filled rivers lined with willows and aspens.

They stopped on a bluff above a small township and took in the panorama of the land. Chace gently pulled up his horse's head to stop it munching the long grass. Then relenting for a moment, slid off the saddle and let the horse eat while he rolled a smoke. Jamie surveyed the town closely through Chace's spyglass. There was plenty of life on the town's boardwalks and the largest street was busy with carts, buckboards and buggies. There were stacks of lumber everywhere and several buildings under construction. Jamie said it looked a thriving community, as he handed Chace the 'scope.

Chace scanned up and down the buildings until his eye alighted on a good-looking hotel, Vendel's. Taking the reins back over the horse's head, he mounted up and steered a steady path down through the pines. Chace had a good feeling. This town in the midst of its struggling expansion didn't look that different from the half-dozen others they had passed through in the last couple of months. It was also far enough away from the inhospitable deserts of Arizona and Utah, where cactus or snakes or outlaws were ready to snag you at every turn. Now they were on the edge of better cattle country, a place full of trees and hills, but on the borders of Indian territory, not to mention bears and wolves. Nowhere in the west was without its dangers.

'We're going to hole up here for a while,' he said over his shoulder to Jamie. 'We'll see how the land lies. I need to make more enquiries. Remember, say nothing about Tom or anything I told you.'

Chace tied the pinto to the hitching rail outside the hotel, while Jamie sat on his own horse with his string of nine others clustered around him. Chace went into the hotel to check in. Jamie cast his eyes up and down the street. It sure was a busy little place, and soon a man, with his thumbs stuck into the top of his gunbelt, came up to Jamie.

'You look kinda young for a bounty hunter, sonny.'

'I ain't no bounty hunter, mister.'

'Whose horses are these then? They look like they don't exactly belong to you, what with their saddles and packs and scabbards an' all. They look like they've been taken away from their rightful owners.'

'They have, an' now they're all legally mine,' Jamie asserted.

Getting a bit anxious, 'Then you must be a bounty hunter, an' like I said, you look a bit young for that.'

Jamie sighed – even sitting on his horse he could smell the whiskey on the man's breath and he didn't want any trouble, having only just arrived in town. 'Well then, you'd better talk to my partner about it, if you're so mighty interested, Mr Pokenose.'

'Ain't no call for that language, sonny. You should show a bit of respect.' He slowly lifted his gun out of its holster and just held it casually, pointing down to the ground. 'Now how about you get yourself down off that nag and let me take a look at the brands. We don't take too kind to horse thieves in these parts.'

Jamie was anxious. 'I wouldn't trouble yourself mister, or you might regret it. They're legally mine and I've got the papers to prove it.' This was, of course, true for the horses which had been signed over by the sheriff in Platt's Cut, but not for the other three from Porky and his two accomplices. Jamie would have to keep bluffing until Chace showed up.

A couple of passers-by had now stopped on the board-walk to see what was going on. A small crowd was beginning to gather, not least because the man was holding a drawn pistol.

'Well, get your paperwork and come to the sheriff's office with me,' the man demanded.

'I've got to stay here with the horses,' Jamie said, now getting desperate.

'You needn't worry about that sonny, there ain't no horse thieves here in Black Creek, 'cept maybe you. They'll be safe enough if you hitch them here, now come on.'

'What's the problem?' demanded Chace's voice behind the man. But before he could look, the man felt the cold, round end of Chace's gun barrel pressing against the side of his head, and a very loud click in his ear as the firing pin was cocked. Chace reached down and eased the pistol out of the man's hand. He gave it up without a struggle and slowly raised his hands half way to show he didn't intend to fight.

'I said you might regret it,' Jamie reminded him. 'Now you can accuse my partner of being a horse thief, if you've got the guts.'

'A horse thief?' Chace repeated, coming round to the front. He emptied all six chambers of the man's gun into

105

the dust and gave it back to him, then holstered his own. 'You'd best put that away and keep it out of my sight unless you know how to use it. And if you want to accuse me of being a horse thief you'd better say it now good an' loud in front of all these fine folk, so we've got witnesses.'

The man smacked his lips, which had gone dry, and sucked in a breath of air to dilute the whiskey fumes, but he didn't say anything.

Chace gave him a withering look. 'Well, mister, I suggest you give up the liquor for a while if it makes you so brave that you go around picking on young lads, and drawing a gun on innocent people. In fact, I better look after your gun for a while.' Chace snatched the gun faster than the man could stop him. 'I guess when you're feeling a little more friendly you can come and apologize for your behaviour and I'll give you back your gun. We'll be staying here a while in Vendel's Hotel, so any time you like. . . . Now get out of my sight.'

The man was still rolling his tongue round his mouth, but it couldn't get hold of any useful words. His eyes were blazing with hatred as he melted into the crowd and disappeared.

A man in the crowd touched Chace's arm. 'You'd better be careful now, mister. That weren't wise.'

'You cut that a bit fine,' Jamie complained.

'I was watching to see what he was going to do. I would have intervened sooner if necessary, don't you worry. There's nothing to fear, I'm looking after you Jamie, you've kinda become one of my responsibilities.' Although those were comforting words for Jamie, they actually meant a lot more to Chace. He unhitched his pinto and mounted up. 'Let's get these into livery, then we can settle ourselves down.'

On the way back from the livery they looked in at the sheriff's office.

'My name's Chace Hexx and this is my young partner, Jamie,' he said shaking the sheriff's hand. 'I took this gun from a drunken troublemaker a moment ago. I'd like you to look after it.'

'Yes, I heard about that. Sheriff Cody Lowe's the name and you're welcome to Black Creek, Mister Hexx, you too, Jamie. I guess you were lucky. The Dagetts kinda own this town. Bart's a dangerous man.

'Throws his weight around and nobody dare touch him. He's no fun when he's had too much whiskey. Ran against me for sheriff couple years back, and still thinks he oughta be the main lawman hereabouts. Taking his gun was a risky thing and I'll gladly look after it. But I'd advise you to watch your back. You've made a powerful enemy. Anyways, have a seat.'

Chace sat down opposite the sheriff while Jamie perched on a bench under the window.

'Just to let you know that all the horses belong to us as a result of dealing with some outlaws and bandits down south. We're not bounty hunters, they're legitimate booty. I have some reward money which I intend using to buy some decent land round here where I can raise some beeves, and Jamie's going to raise horses. Can you recommend an honest land agent in the town?'

'Well, there ain't no government land available here right now – if you want that you gotta head north to Wyoming, or east to Nebraska, plenty going there. But as it happens, Bart Dagett's brother has a big spread just a little ways north of the town, an' I heard he's looking to sell up. Aaron Sindersen is a decent land agent, go an' have a word with him.'

They took their leave of the sheriff and crossed to the hotel. Unpacking their bags, Chace said, 'I have a nasty feeling about that Bart Dagett. Could be a coincidence, Bart being his name. Anyway, our first call tomorrow morning will be that land agent, Aaron Sindersen. If there's good land going I want to go and see it. Right now, we'd better get ourselves cleaned up and get something to eat.'

That night, Jamie turned in early, being seduced by the soft feather bed and clean sheets. The weariness of the last few weeks of constant trekking had finally caught up with him, and he'd struggled to keep his eyes open during dinner while eating his pie. After he'd gone up, Chace went into the hotel's saloon, ordered a beer, and took a seat at a table. He rolled himself a smoke and settled down for a quiet evening watching the local people. It wasn't long before a flighty young lady approached him. She pulled out a chair, preparing to sit down.

'May I join you?' she asked politely, with a smile and disarming flicker of her eyelids. She didn't wait for an answer, but sat herself down comfortably in it. 'You're new into town, aren't you, Chace? I may call you Chace, mayn't I?'

'Er, yes ma'am,' Chace replied with a furrowed brow. 'That's correct, I'm new here and my name is Chace, and you're welcome to use it.'

'Yes, I know Mr Hexx. After all, it's my job to know all the guests in the hotel.' She reached her hand across the table. 'I'm Bryony Vendel, Mrs Bryony Vendel, and this is my hotel. I saw you ride in, and I was intrigued by the number of horses you brought into town, and a boy as well, and I thought I'd like to know a little bit more about you. I watched you check in. I like your quiet confidence,

108

Mr Hexx. A man who carries a six-gun and looks like he knows how to handle it.'

Chace smiled, then remembered his manners. 'Can I get you a drink?'

'No need,' Bryony replied. She looked over her shoulder and whistled to the bar tender. He immediately poured a shot of amber liquid and another glass of beer. They were brought across to the table. She raised her glass to Chace. 'Good health Mr Hexx, and welcome to Black Creek.'

'Good health, ma'am.'

'Well now, Chace, may I ask you what your business is here in the Creek?'

'As a matter of fact I've come to buy myself a spread and raise the best beef this side of Kentucky.'

She smiled, 'Oh, have you now? And what about your boy, I suppose he'll work on the ranch as well?'

'Yes and no. He's not my boy, and he'll be doing his own thing with horses.'

'He's not your boy . . .'

'No, he isn't, but he feels a lot like it. Anyway, it's a long story and I'm kinda responsible for him.'

'Gee, you're young to be having a responsibility like that. Why, for goodness sakes, you must be about the same age as me, and I'm much too young to have children.'

Chace knew his manners well enough neither to take her seriously nor to enquire into the young lady's age, but he felt she was being a touch provocative. 'But not too young to own a hotel,' he said, rather probingly.

'That's a long story,' she said with a sigh and a shrug of her neat shoulders, which were nicely revealed by her fine silk décolletage dress. 'I'm more than happy to listen to your story, if you'll let me tell you mine.'

'I'm all ears,' said Chace, leaning forward in an interested manner.

Bryony laughed, 'Don't mock, Mr Hexx. Anyways, I might need your services.'

'My services?'

'I heard you're a bounty hunter, is that not so?'

Chace shook his head. 'No ma'am, that is definitely not so.'

'Then how come you have so many horses?'

'I only have one, the others belong to the boy.'

Bryony smiled and paused. She looked at Chace wistfully because she knew he was prevaricating. 'Seven horses? And how did he get them?'

'I gave them to him,' Chace looked her straight in the eye, then corrected himself. 'Actually he earned them, all bar one which his pa gave him.'

'You're being mighty cagey about this, if I may say so,' she said. 'You don't get fully furnished horses, gun scabbards an' all, without a fight of some sort. I don't think you're a cattle man, more like a gunfighter.'

'You think so?'

'Listen, Mr Hexx, for whatever reason, I see something in you I like. Now it don't do for men to follow me up the stairs, but I want you to come to my room in, say, ten minutes' time, top floor.' She stood up to go and gave him a little nod of the head to show that she expected to be obeyed. Chace simply lifted his glass and took a swig.

He ordered another beer. Two things were for sure, he wasn't at anybody's beck and call however pretty they might be, and he didn't want anyone thinking he was a bounty hunter. Having cleared that with himself he decided it would be very ill-mannered not to visit the lady proprietor as requested. He finished his beer, ran his sleeve across his lips, and went out into the street.

Stars twinkled at him from a cloudless, inky-black sky. He sat down on a bench and wanted to roll a smoke, but decided he didn't have time for that. He'd heard somewhere that it didn't do to keep ladies waiting. He sucked in deeply, then blew out some air, sounding almost like a horse. He didn't realize it was symptomatic of plucking up the courage to visit the top floor. He went in through the hotel entrance, mounted the wide staircase two at a time, crossed two landings to the top floor and was confronted with several doors. Just one of them had a name: The Dagett Suite. Dagett? So somehow the hotel was connected to Bart Dagett – but that didn't make a whole lot of sense. Or did it? Chace was about to knock, when he heard raised voices arguing inside the room. He waited until there was silence, then knocked gently.

'Come in!'

He opened the door. At the same moment, Bryony closed another door at the far side of the room and came towards him. She sat down on a *chaise longue*. The room glowed with candlelight reflected from the polished wood panelling, and absorbed into the heavy crimson velvet curtains. There was a heady scent of sweet orange perfume. The gilded woodwork on the furniture gave an air of opulence. It was all very enticing.

'Come in,' Bryony repeated, patting the cushion beside her. 'I don't bite!'

Chace closed the door and sat himself down comfortably in the place she indicated.

'I like candles,' she said. 'They're warmer and more comforting than gas lights, and I prefer them at night.'

'It's a real nice room.'

'I keep the whole of the top floor for myself,' she said.

'I like the space. Reminds me of the great open plains when we used to have our own ranch.'

'You have a ranch?'

'Not any more. We started out like that, Mr Loevendel and me. . . .'

'He lives here too?' Chace asked, before she had finished her sentence. It sounded a bit too interested.

Bryony shook her head, 'Mr Loevendel is buried in Nebraska. Two years ago in '74 we had just got our farm going. Hundred and sixty acres of government grazing land. It was just before the Pawnee were persuaded on to a government reservation. Up to then we'd had very few problems with Indians. I guess we were just lucky. Then despite being usually peaceful when left alone, a renegade group of Pawnee decided to burn out some settlers, and we just happened to be one of the ranches they picked on. They were mad at the Sioux and mad at the government, and we were just in the way of their anger. Anyway, that's how my husband lost his life, defending his home and me.'

Chace gave Bryony a searching look. 'And you?'

'I was hidden in a safe place under the house, so escaped the violence. Afterwards I had no choice really – I couldn't face that kind of life without my man, so I packed up and left.'

There was a silence that Chace couldn't fill; he didn't want to pry into Bryony's past, and she didn't seem to want to say any more about it. But he had to ask: 'His name was Loevendel, yours is Vendel, you said.'

'Gustav was a German immigrant, I just changed my name a bit, to move on.' She quickly changed the subject: 'How much would you charge to kill a man?'

'Hey, I'm no murderer, nor a bounty hunter, I already

told you that.'

'I know you did,' she said, with a disarming smile, 'but you're not a very good liar, Chace – you've killed men, I can see it in your eyes. You shouldn't ever take up poker, you can be read as easy as an open book!'

'Well, if you can read men that easy, perhaps you should play poker yourself, you'd make a fortune.'

'And get myself shot? Poker's for suckers. Anyway, I've got a good business in the hotel.'

The awkward silence descended into the room again and Chace wished it would go away, but he kept thinking about what she was asking.

She put her hand on his knee and drew a small circle. 'I'm serious, you know. I'm in danger, and I need someone who can shoot straight.'

Chace made no reply. Bryony continued to trace a circle on his knee. 'I guess you can at least shoot straight?'

'Why don't you go and see Sheriff Lowe? There must be a dozen men would help you out at the click of your fingers and pretty smile.'

It was the first time he'd used the word 'pretty' with Bryony. His cheeks coloured up fast because it had just slipped out. He'd had no intention of letting on that he thought she was one of the most attractive women he had ever seen. Especially while one of her dainty fingers was running round his knee. He hoped the candlelight would hide his embarrassment.

'An' there's more than a dozen men would swoon at my feet if I asked them a favour,' she countered. 'Why are you so different?'

'I'm no different, ma'am. I just came here to get away from that kind of thing an' start a new life.' Which was partly true.

'Aha!' she exclaimed triumphantly, getting up with a swish of her dress. She crossed to a sideboard stacked with bottles and glasses. 'I knew it. A woman's intuition, Mr Hexx! You see, Chace, I just knew you were the man I was waiting for. Whiskey?' She poured him a tumblerful without waiting for an answer. She handed him the glass, and instead of sitting down on the *chaise longue*, took her glass and sat in a large armchair a little further away. She was more experienced at fishing than any man with a rod and line. She'd shown Chace the bait and was just waiting to strike.

'What kind of danger?' he asked at last, after he'd taken a couple of swallows of the whiskey.

Bryony widened her eyes at him. 'Mortal danger. He'll want to kill me an' maybe burn down the hotel.'

'That's one hell of a grudge. . . .'

Getting up quickly, Bryony put her glass down on a delicate little mahogany tripod table. She crossed the room to one of the doors and put her hand on the door handle, then turned to Chace. 'Would you mind giving me a moment while I change into something less formal?' She opened the door and Chace could see a huge four-poster bed with rich velvet drapes. 'I won't be long.' She didn't close the door but disappeared from view.

Chace turned the glass round in his hand. What was he getting himself into? He'd already crossed swords with Bart Dagett, and the sheriff had added his warning. Now maybe he was encroaching on Bart's property. In a way he didn't really care too much, but he had a responsibility for Jamie, and he had to take that into account. In any case it was highly unlikely he'd be drawn into some kind of feud on Bryony's behalf. More than likely she sized up all her guests just to get to know them. But as he took another swig of the whiskey, he realized that that was a ridiculous thought – she wouldn't be doing this kind of entertaining with everyone.

'Chace, could you give me a hand? I can't undo the lace. I think I pulled it too hard and the end has gotten caught.' She backed herself towards the door and stood there with one hand over her shoulder plucking at the recalcitrant lace, the other holding her corset in place. Her knee-length frilly cotton drawers had pink ribbons entwined round the waist and delicately woven in and out down the side seam and above the hem. She was wearing fine black stockings and her shoes gleamed with delicate cut steel buckles. Chace tried to avert his eyes, but had to look to see where the lace had tangled itself. He pulled it free and went back to his whiskey. Bryony emerged in a pink silk dressing-gown. This time she sat down next to Chace on the *chaise longue.*

'Just say you'll do it, and I'll tell you all about it. You won't regret it, I promise. When you've heard what he did you'll want to kill him anyway, and you'll find me a warm and generous person. I think you need me as much as I need you.'

'What makes you think that?'

She smiled, running her hand gently over Chace's cheek and round his chin. 'A woman's intuition.'

11

The mixture of whiskey, candlelight and perfume was a heady concoction. Added to the long day's ride, it all conspired to make Chace feel quite drowsy. He sank back into the soft plush of the upholstery. Bryony tucked one leg underneath the other and rested her arm along the polished mahogany back. Chace could almost feel the warmth of her body and found himself strangely confused in this physically comfortable, but rather unfamiliar territory.

'After I buried my husband, I wanted to stay on and make something of the life we had started together. But I couldn't manage a hundred and sixty acres on my own, and I kinda knew I had to give it up. So I sold up for next to nothing – after all, it was government land grab – and I drifted into a two-bit town where I could get some work in a saloon. I mean, what else is there for a young woman to do? I served drinks, I sang a bit and danced, I got paid very little, but at least I had meals and a roof over my head. Then . . . well, you know how it is, it was a kinda run down sort of place and sooner or later some big shot turned up and offered me the chance to sing on a proper stage in a big bustling town. A star in the making.'

'And so you went with him?'

'Sure did. I was so naïve. He said he was recruiting and took the whole troupe of us, six girls. All the way down south to Texas where he had a saloon and theatre.'

'And then the dancing turned out to be something else.'

'Not for a while,' she said, shaking her head. 'I thought I was going to be the talk of the town, the desert rose of the show. The hotel he owned was a big one, and there were a whole lot of dancing girls. Far from being the star performer, I was just a nobody in the chorus line. I hated it. I wanted to get away, but it isn't that easy for a woman with no money and nobody to look out for her.'

'Haven't you got any family?'

'Back east near Springfield, but my parents were disappointed when I wanted to marry Gustav, the man I loved. Being good, honest, God-fearing folk they'd given me a good education and hoped I was going to be a school teacher or something like that. Gustav wanted to be a farmer. It was a big let-down for them. They sort of gave their blessing, but washed their hands of me at the same time. We married and got some land out west in Nebraska.'

Bryony lapsed into a long period of quiet, no doubt thinking about her family, the life she had left, and the way all her hopes and dreams had been shattered. She got up and filled their glasses. 'You see, Chace, I can tell you've had some disappointment like mine. I can see it in your eyes. It leaves its mark.'

'It does,' he said. 'Deep down it hurts. Only for me it was the other way round. I washed my family out of my life, because of the war. That last day in the spring of '65. I'll never forget it. General Lee made a desperate attempt

117

to break out of the tunnels and ditches, but it ended in disaster. I was only sixteen. I took a slug in the shoulder and collapsed. Moments later my best friend, Henck Peerson, fell dead across my body, a bullet through his forehead. In blind panic I somehow escaped with the rest of Lee's army. I broke away with other disillusioned soldiers to fight small-scale skirmishes, killing everyone we could find wearing a dark blue uniform. A few weeks later, the Confederacy capitulated and the war was over.

'I went home to find my parents. They were embittered and utterly changed. My two sisters had been violated by Yankee troopers. I was changed too, and I turned my back on them all and left for good.' He sighed deeply.

'What happened then?'

'I drifted. I moved from ranch to ranch – cattle, horses, took any work I could get. Wasting my life. Now, look at me. Always been good with a gun, but only in self-defence or to uphold the law. The law as I see it, anyways. But I don't want to get used to killing folk. I turned down work as a deputy.'

'And if you help me out, you're afraid you might slide down that slippery slope towards bounty hunting.'

Chace shook his head and turned the glass round in his hand, thinking how to put it. 'No, not exactly. I've got to look after Jamie, and well, yes, you're right there'll always be just one more job to do, one more killing. One more injustice to avenge. It'll never stop and I've done enough. Well, nearly. Now I want to finish things off and live peaceful, raise some beef, settle down, maybe have a wife and children of my own. That's what ordinary folk do, isn't it?'

Bryony sensed that Chace needed to get something out of his memory. It was obvious there was something he'd rather forget, and she knew the best way to start getting rid of the past is to confront it, not ignore it.

'Tell me what happened after you left home.'

'It ain't that interesting.'

'I'll decide about that,' she said. 'I want to hear it.'

'You do? Well, for the next twelve years I tried to forget everything in a life of drifting. There wasn't anything illegal, but I practised shooting endlessly until I became highly dangerous with a six-gun and a rifle. Then I fell in with other drifters and cattle drivers and quickly learned the art of fist fighting and wrestling. In a little over a year and still only seventeen I had turned from being an idealistic upstanding youth into a hardened cowpoke. I became part of a small itinerant band moving from ranch to ranch, working the seasons.

'Eventually I left them, and drifted into Arizona where I worked at a livery. That's where I was approached by a man named Tom Purdy. He was a few years older than me, a rancher and a lawman. He was on the trail of a gang wanted for murder, robbery and worse. I was beginning to see the pointlessness of my life, and helping Tom was going to give me a new direction. Tom quickly became a good friend, a man I could admire and trust, the kind of person I really wanted to be. But it all went wrong.' Chace was silent, his chin sunk on his chest.

Bryony prompted him to continue. 'How so?'

'A violent end. A miscalculation. Tom was killed by the men he'd been tracking for two years. They had violated his wife and then killed her with his child. He had to watch it all. He was a part-time Texas Ranger, and they stole his badge. He caught up with them at a ranch in Arizona, but he must have been recognized and was bludgeoned to death by the gang. He'd given me the lowdown on a raid the gang were planning, and with that information I shot three of them while they were robbing a bank, but too late to save an innocent young woman who lost her life.'

The back of his eyes started to smart and he put up his hand to make sure a tear didn't form, but Bryony was watching him closely. She laid her hand softly on him. 'There's a lot of sadness there, Chace. Don't try to hold it back.'

'It's silly really, I just keep losing people.' He composed himself. 'Well, I finished Tom's mission by shooting down the Rees gang as they tried to rob a bank. Then a short time later I got involved in a stagecoach robbery and killed three more outlaws. That's where I picked up Jamie. His pa was the driver, shot dead by the robbers. More death, more loss.'

'And now you feel a responsibility towards Jamie. Maybe you're helping to take away some of his loss.'

'Maybe. I hadn't thought of it like that.'

'Didn't you have a sweetheart at all?'

Chace snorted a sharp exhalation of breath, 'Not really, until I drifted into that livery. Just casual, prior to that. Roseanne was the daughter of the livery owner. I liked her a lot. Probably more than I realized at the time. Even asked her to come away with me.'

'But you lost her too?'

'No. . . . Well, in a way, yes, but I understood why she couldn't leave her pa.'

'It was another loss, Chace.'

He thought for a moment. 'Yeah. I guess you're right. Just another loss.'

'You see,' Bryony said, more cheerfully. 'I told you we need each other.'

She knew she'd hooked him, and it was only a matter of time playing the line until the fish tired and gave in; then she would reel him in. 'It's getting late. I need some sleep. Promise you'll come back and talk some more tomorrow night?'

Chace got slowly to his feet and stretched. 'If you want.'

They crossed to the door and she opened it for him, but not wide enough for him to leave. She reached up and kissed his cheek lightly, then opened the door wider, smiled, and gently pushed him out.

The sun was streaming in through the open window when Chace woke up the next morning. Jamie, already dressed, was gently shaking him, 'Chace, Chace, time to wake up. I've got you some coffee. A cup of good strong coffee. Mrs Vendel says you're to join her for breakfast.'

'What?'

Jamie wafted the cup under Chace's nose to try and entice his eyelids to open. 'Here, drink this, you know you don't become human until you've had your coffee.'

'Yeah, right.'

'I'll tell Mrs Vendel you're on your way.'

Jamie made off, closing the door behind him. Chace's eyes opened. He ran his hand through his dishevelled hair and then round the stubble on his chin. Throwing back the sheets he sat on the side of the bed in his longjohns. It wouldn't do to keep Mrs Vendel waiting, and how come she was up so early herself? He reached out a hand to fumble for his pocket watch on the night stand. It was nearly nine o'clock. Not so early after all. Splashing some cold water on his face brought him instantly to life. He pulled on his shirt and woollen trousers, buckled his belt, brushed his teeth, spat out of the window, wetted, dried and arranged his hair to look presentable, pulled on his boots, tied a bandanna round his neck, and made his way downstairs. He went straight out through the hotel door into the street, sucked in some good cold fresh air and went back in through the saloon batwings where he saw Bryony and Jamie sitting at a table.

'Good mornin', Chace, cook is doing you some steak an' eggs to get you fired up.' She picked up the coffee pot and poured out a cup. 'Jamie says you need at least two cups before you can talk in the morning.'

'Hmm,' was as much of a reply that Chace could manage.

Jamie smiled at Bryony. 'You see what I mean, ma'am.'

She set the cup down in front of Chace. 'Jamie tells me you're going to see Aaron Sindersen, the land agent. I expect he'll tell you the Dagett place is up for sale. May even want to take you out there. Don't go. The Dagetts are unpredictable. What you done to Bart was no more 'an he deserved, but his brother looks out for him an' he won't have taken too kindly to you humiliatin' him. He'll see it as a slur on his family name, and the Dagetts are a bit of a big noise round here. Bull is likely to run for mayor next election, and Bart ran for sheriff last time out.'

The cup stopped on its way to Chace's mouth. Did he hear right? Did she say Bull? Bull running for mayor? Bart and Bull. The cup continued its journey.

Having drunk his second cup of coffee Chace was feeling a little more awake, but found he didn't really have much to say, as he was deep in thought.

Realizing conversation with Chace would be tantamount to flogging a dead horse, Bryony continued the conversation with Jamie. 'So how did you meet Chace exactly, you said something earlier about it being at the point of a gun?'

'Yes ma'am, I had a gun barrel pressed against my head.'

So began Jamie's brief account, which continued while Chace ate his steak and eggs, washed it down with yet another cup of coffee, then leaned back in his chair with his arms behind his head, until Jamie's narrative reached the point where he and Chace had arrived at Vendel's Hotel.

Bryony turned to Chace. 'It seems mighty generous to give Jamie all those horses.'

Chace shrugged. 'Everyone needs a little help to get started.' He got up from his chair. 'Now if you'll excuse us, ma'am, we need to get started on our search for some land.'

A short while later they reached Aaron Sindersen's office and introduced themselves.

Sindersen's podgy white hands rested nervously on the edge of his desk, as if he were holding it back. 'Take a seat, Mr Hexx, and you Jamie, I've heard a lot about you already. Coffee?'

'I'd rather get straight to the point,' said Chace.

The flabby fingers lifted themselves into the air acknowledging the refusal of hospitality. 'I understand you're looking for some land. Sheriff Lowe said you might be interested in the Dagett spread.'

'Did he really?' Chace said casually, noting how quickly news travelled in a close-knit community.

Jamie gave Chace a quick glance. 'Mrs Vendel said . . .'

Chace rapidly finished Jamie's sentence, '. . . it would be worth a look.'

'Good,' said Sindersen, bringing his hands together in

a prayer-like shape. 'I'll take you out there myself.'

'There's no need for that,' Chace said firmly. 'Just point us in the right direction.'

'Well, if you're sure. Take the road out north for about two miles and you'll find the Dagett spread signposted on the right by a fingerboard pointing to the Bar BBD. It might be better if I came with you. . . .'

Chace got up to leave and Jamie followed suit. As they got to the door Chace turned to the agent and asked 'What did Sheriff Lowe say to you about my encounter yesterday with Bart Dagett?'

Sindersen put his hand up to his face and stroked his chin. 'I don't remember that being spoken of.'

'Oh,' Chace said, as he opened the door. When they got outside he turned to Jamie. 'We need to be careful, that was a bare-faced lie. The Bar BBD needs checking out. I rather wish I hadn't made an enemy of Bull Dagett.'

'Don't you mean Bart?'

'He's a four flush. Bull's the one running for mayor. He won't be chicken feed like his brother. I'm looking forward to meeting him.'

Half an hour later they were heading for the Dagett spread. Chace either doffed his hat or raised his hand to the passing buckboards, buggies and occasional lone riders and received courteous acknowledgment in return.

'Black Creek seems a nice enough place to me,' he said to Jamie, as they ambled along the busy road. 'The folk are friendly. The land looks good. What do you think?'

'I'm still worried. Mrs Vendel said not to go to the Dagett ranch, so why are we headed out that way?'

'Same reason moths dance by the firelight.'

That didn't help Jamie a whole lot, and he fell into a pondering silence. The sun was rising into the clear blue sky. The wind played a rustling tune on the aspen leaves. A blue jay warned of the riders' presence, and high above the pine woods a big bird of prey took advantage of the thermals, proclaiming its dominance with an eerie, plaintiff call. Chace had a good feeling about Black Creek. He had a good feeling about Bryony Vendel. He even had a strong feeling about Bull Dagett. Surely these Dagett brothers must be Tom Purdy's quarry from Texas. The Bull and Bart name coincidence was too strong, and Dagett was a simple change of Hagen at the beginning and end. The lead he'd been given was coming up trumps. But he also knew that when you feel too good about everything, something bad has a nasty habit of spoiling it.

'I've got a hunch there might be trouble at the Dagett place, and I don't want to put you in any danger, Jamie.'

'I'm not letting you go in there alone.'

'That's big talk, and you better be careful chucking your weight around like that, because you ain't got much more'n a hundred pounds of it! Nevertheless, I appreciate the sentiment. Listen, we play it absolutely cool – remember we're here to buy land.'

They soon came to the track Aaron Sindersen had described. After a short distance they passed under the big pine gateway emblazoned with large letters cut into the wood and painted bright red, announcing 'Dagett Ranch – Bar BBD.'

The track wound its way through a good stand of mature broad-leaved trees until it emerged at the head of a broad valley, watered by a winding river away to the east. The grassland stretched away in all directions, and grazing cattle could be seen far into the distance where the countryside was dotted with numerous outcrops rising

125

into a distant ridge of reddish mountains. The substantial ranch house and cluster of other buildings were nestled neatly into the fold of the land and sheltered by a stand of young cottonwood.

'Well, Jamie, can you see yourself in a place like this? I'll bet there's more'n a thousand acres here.'

'We'd never manage all that on our own. I thought we were going to start small and see how things went along?'

'Sometimes you have to bite the bullet. Think small and you'll stay small. You want a big herd of horses, don't you?'

'I want to try breeding – my pa was always talking about improving the stock by breeding, only I don't know exactly how I'd go about it, or what I have to do.'

Just then a couple of riders emerged from behind them. 'Hold it right there and don't do nuthin' quick or silly, Mr Tinhorn Hexx.'

'Hello Bart,' Chace said, without turning round. 'We're not here to do nothin' silly. Aaron Sindersen sent us here to look at the ranch. Bull wants to sell, I believe.'

'No way,' replied Bart Dagett. 'Not to the likes of you, anyway, even if you had enough dough to buy.' He rode round to the front, a six-gun in his hand. His partner remained behind and out of sight, but Chace could sense the barrels of a shotgun.

'Looks like a nice spread you got here. Why are you selling up?'

Chace's unflustered manner allowed the tension to ease up a little.

'Bull's had enough of ranching, wants to expand his hotel business, he's building three more already, one in Black Creek and another two about fifty miles away in Burton's Bluff.'

'You said he wants to expand, so he's got a hotel already?'

'And a woman to go with it, but that's his business not yours. I think you seen enough for one day, so just turn around and ride out, mister. You can tell Aaron we ain't sellin' to you, so there ain't no point in lookin' no further. Got it?'

'Got it,' Chace repeated. 'Let's just turn around and ride out, Jamie. Some other day we'll get to talk to the organ grinder, not the monkey.'

Bart Dagett leant across and smacked Chace's chin with his handgun. 'Watch yer tongue, Hexx, or I'll put a hole through it.'

The blow smarted, but Chace knew Bart was gutless and wouldn't dare pull the trigger with the boy as a witness, unless he really was cowardly enough to shoot a boy as well. Chace had a hunch it was Bull who ruled the roost anyway. So he calmly turned his horse, and they both rode back up to the main track.

Breathing a sigh of relief, Jamie said, 'Phew, I thought that was going to turn nasty.'

'No sweat,' Chace reassured him, stroking his chin. 'Just a pair of cowpokes.'

'That was Bart, Bull Dagett's brother, isn't it? The man who tried to march me off to the sheriff?'

'That's him all right, and he blabbered some useful information for me. Let's head back to town.'

They passed the afternoon mooching. Chace paid a visit to the barber to get a shave, and they spent an hour or so grooming their horses. Jamie was in his element but Chace was chewing over some awkward details. He couldn't help coming back time and again to the question of why Bryony wanted him to track down some fellow giving her trouble. He could feel bits of a puzzle swirling in his mind, but no clear connection between the pieces. What made her think he'd commit murder for her, and why had she latched on to him the moment he set foot in town? Last night had been a very comfortable time spent in her suite. He knew he wouldn't be able to resist the perfume, the candlelight and a pretty woman.

He watched Jamie oiling the hoofs on one of the horses. How simple everything is when you're thirteen. But then on reflection he realized life was just as complicated for Jamie, perhaps more so, because he didn't have the wherewithal to control his own destiny. Almost like a baby, he was utterly dependent on another human being. Whatever else Chace did, he was determined not to let Jamie down.

It was a busy evening in the hotel, and the saloon was full to bursting. A pianist thrashed some familiar tunes out of the ivories, the card tables were full and there was a general air of good-natured enjoyment. Jamie went up to bed quite early and Chace joined in a poker table. He lost near a hundred dollars but he wasn't really bothered; in any case he wasn't thinking about the cards. At one point he had been so distracted thinking about Bryony that he had folded with a pair of eights in his hand and another one turned up on the table. He could probably have won a pile of dollars with three of a kind.

It was this lack of concentration, more than the loss of dollars, which made him realize it was time to stop playing. With the consent of the other players, he scooped up what was left of his cash and went outside for a smoke. It was getting late, and he would soon have to decide whether to visit Bryony as requested. Then he remembered she'd made him promise, so there wasn't a choice.

Deep in thought and taking in the cool air he wandered round the back of the hotel, puffing out small streams of blue-tinged tobacco smoke as he exhaled into the night. But at just that moment a door flew open at the top of the fire escape and a figure came flying down, his boots clattering on the wooden treads. Having come out of a lighted room into the dark, the man's eyes had obviously not adjusted and he ran full pelt into Chace, knocking him clean off his feet. Before Chace could fathom what had happened, the figure had disappeared like a wraith into the shadows. Looking up, Chace with his perfectly adjusted night eyes, could see the door was still open. He climbed the stairs, and on the top step, realized it must lead into Bryony's suite.

'Bryony?' he said, in not much more than a whisper. 'Bryony, are you in there?'

There was no reply. Slowly, he eased himself inside. Moonlight provided a dull glimmer through the uncurtained windows. There was no other light. He was in a large parlour, not the one he'd been in the night before – this was a different part of Bryony's suite. A small table lay on its side where it had been knocked over. He stood the table up and proceeded with caution, having no idea what might be going on in the next room. He stood by the door, listening for any conversation, but there was none. It felt eerily quiet. He drew his gun, turned the handle, and slowly opened the door.

12

The scene that greeted him was not good. He holstered his gun and went to the chaise longue where Bryony was lying, half on and half off. Her hair was dishevelled, the top of her dress was ripped, one shoe was off, and there was a trickle of blood in the corner of her mouth. Her eyelids flickered. Gently he moved her back on to the seat. He went into the bedroom and returned with a cloth he'd dipped into the water basin. He gently wiped the corner of her mouth, straightened out her dress and took off her other shoe. Going to the sideboard he searched amongst the bottles for the brandy, and poured a slug, which he put to her lips.

Her eyes opened a fraction, but there was no focus to them. 'Who are you?'

'It's Chace, and you're safe now. Don't try to talk, just take another sip.'

He went into the bedroom and brought back a quilt blanket, which he tucked round her. He gave her another slug of the brandy.

'It's the strangest feeling,' she said weakly, running her hand across her forehead, 'coming out of the black hole of unconsciousness. It's by no means the first time, but it never gets any easier.'

'What d'you mean, it's not the first time?'

She shrugged. 'I used to get knocked about a lot, you get used to it.'

'No woman should ever get used to it.'

Bryony sighed, and finished off the drink. She held out the glass to Chace. 'Give me another one, Chace. A proper drink, not a medicinal spoonful this time.' Coming back to life, she eased herself into a sitting position. 'You'd make a good medical orderly. There's a very caring side to you, isn't there? Despite your toughness.'

He handed her a proper-sized glass. 'Just doing what anyone would.' He paused as she took a gulp. 'Is all this to do with you wanting me to get rid of someone for you?'

'In a way, yes.'

'And is this violence likely to happen again?'

She hesitated. 'Yes. Look, don't take this the wrong way, but now it includes you.'

'Me? What do you mean?'

Bryony put her hand on her chin and felt round both jaws. 'Nothing broken I'm glad to say, just the little cut inside my mouth. It all looks worse than it is. Was I out for long?'

'I don't think so,' Chace reassured her. 'I was up the fire escape pretty fast after he left. Who was it anyway, and how does it include me?'

'Not important . . .'

'Not important?' Chace repeated, incredulously. 'Some maniac comes careering down the fire escape, crashes into me in his rush to get away having knocked you unconscious, and you say it's not important?'

'It isn't really. Won't you come and sit down? I hadn't finished telling you my story last night.' Chace made himself comfortable on the end of the *chaise longue*. She tried to smile at him, but her face hurt. 'You were going to come back tonight anyway, weren't you?'

Chace didn't admit that he'd been having second thoughts. 'Of course.'

'Did you and Jamie go and see any land today?'

'Never mind about that,' he said, taking a gulp of whiskey. 'Tell me what's going on. Is it to do with the chorus line?'

'So you did listen carefully. . . .'

He wanted to tell Bryony he was becoming very interested in everything about her, but didn't. 'Of course,' he replied disingenuously. 'It would be ill-mannered not to.'

'Well, eventually the big boss man said he had a leading part for me in a new show if I wanted it. I jumped at the idea. But there was a catch, of course, and he started to make demands. At first it was no more than having a drink with him in his room while he talked about the new songs and the dance routines. . . .'

'But he wanted more than just to talk.'

'Yes, and I refused. So he slapped me about a bit and said I was an ungrateful bitch. Only it didn't stop there. I didn't know what to do. I hadn't got anywhere to go, and I was getting beat up a lot. There were two brothers, wealthy financiers, crooks who were backing his operation, and I was told I had to entertain them as well. I refused and got more beatings. They wanted to break me. Other girls gave in to them, but I was determined not to. They got beatings too, even when they did what was wanted. They cried a lot.

'I was determined not to give in. It would have been so easy to do so. But the more I refused, the more they wanted me. Well, it went on and on until I couldn't stand any more. I wanted to kill all three of them, those brothers and the showman. I started to dream about how I could do it. In some dreams I'd shoot them, in others I'd poison a drink and give it to them. In one dream I hired a young gun to kill them for me.'

'That's beginning to sound familiar,' Chace observed.

Bryony smiled. 'Maybe. But I didn't need to kill them, if I could just get away; but for that I needed money. Well, the long and the short of it is that I stole their money. I knew where the cash was kept, and when I had my opportunity I was flabbergasted. It was bundles and bundles of dollars, far more than the theatre was producing. Anyway, I filled two big saddlebags, took a horse and rode away in the middle of the night. I was so scared I was being followed, it being dark an' all and I could scarce see where I was going. But I rode till the horse was in a lather, and the sound of the hoof-beats matched the pounding of my heart. I was terrified that I was about to hear gunshots at any moment.'

'But you survived.'

'I sure did. I don't think anybody knew I was gone until the next day when both the money and me were missing. That was two years ago, and that's how I bought this hotel and made a new life for myself. I called it Vendel's in memory of my husband.'

'It's a strange thing – I also had trouble with two brothers.' Chace paused, reflecting on the loss of Tom and DeSoto's bank. 'Well, I hope you put many miles between yourself and that theatre manager.'

'I did. He was about to set up a big new variety theatre with those two brothers. They had big plans and loads of money, until I stole it. So I came all the way out here to Black Creek, hoping it was far enough away from Texas.'

Chace stroked his chin. 'Any number of miles is never enough when you've separated a man from his . . .'

'. . . money?' she wondered.

'No, not that. His pride,' Chace corrected. 'Robbed by a woman, and she got away? No man would live that down until he caught her. That's why you want him killed.'

'Not exactly. It's not quite that simple.'

'Oh?' Chace furrowed his brow. 'Oh, I see, don't tell me, it's something to do with you being beat up tonight, isn't it?'

'I invested a lot of money in this hotel, Chace, apart from a considerable stash put aside for a rainy day, and now I stand to lose it all.'

Chace got up off the chaise longue and started pacing around the room. 'The showman's caught up with you. An' you think I'm going to risk my life to save your hotel? No, this don't make a whole lot of sense to me. How is the theatre showman linked to you being beat up tonight? Listen, I've got enough money to buy a ranch and build a hotel as well. Why don't you just give it up here and come with me and the boy? We'll move somewhere a long ways off, there's land going in Montana. They'll need hotels up there as well, might even have some for sale already.'

He had no idea why he'd just made that proposition, another spur of the moment thing, just like with Roseanne. Another insubstantial dream. What was he looking for?

Bryony shook her head. 'That's just it, nowhere would be safe if I went with you.'

'Why's that?'

'This isn't to do with the theatre showman. He'll never find me.'

'What then?'

'Come and sit down and I'll tell you,' she said very softly, in a way she knew Chace couldn't resist. 'You're right, the showman's pride was hurt, but worse still I heard he went bust soon afterwards. You see, the money I stole wasn't really his. It belonged to those two brothers, his financial backers. They had some big business going on in Texas, in fact they were part of a gang of thieves. They were going to build a new town with hotels, saloons and the biggest variety theatre in Texas. But the gang was busted and split up, and these two came north to Colorado looking for me and their money. It was their plans I'd interfered with. A woman with money is something of a rarity, but even so, it took them a while to find me.'

Chace nodded his head. 'And now, after you've got your business going successfully, they want their money back. And if you don't hand it over to them lock, stock and barrel, they'll turn you over.'

'That's about it. I'll have nothing.'

'So it's not a theatre showman you want plugged, it's two big shot financiers!' Chace shook his head. 'It gets worse and worse.'

For a moment Bryony remained silent. She wanted Chace to take it in before she told him the rest. She was conscious there was a point when he might just refuse, and walk out. But then on the other hand, hadn't he just made a sort of proposal to her by saying she could go with him and Jamie, and start afresh somewhere else? Her heart skipped a beat because she knew that emotionally she was somehow attracted to Chace, and the prospect of going anywhere with him seemed infinitely preferable to anything else. But she had to try and stop her heart ruling her head. Chace seemed her best bet in dealing with her present predicament, but a man's promises can easily be broken – the showman had taught her that. Besides, she had no proof that Chace had any money at all, let alone enough to buy a ranch and a hotel. It seemed unlikely. She was playing the line to reel in a big catch, but wasn't sure if she'd only caught a slippery eel.

Having chewed things over, Chace was puzzled. 'You said being beat up was something to do with me. How d'you work that out?'

'He's jealous.'

'Who is?'

'One of the brothers.' Bryony paused and covered her eyes with the back of her hand. 'He knew you were here the other night, in my room.'

'Not for long.'

'Long enough,' she said.

'Hardly.'

'He wants me to marry him.' She blurted it out. 'He's been asking for so long, he wants a decision. Then you turn up and he hears about me talking to you, having breakfast with you, knows you were up here last night . . .'

'And he beats you up for that?'

'I'm used to it. It was Bart Dagett who was here.'

'That jumped up. . .'

'Him and his brother are the two financiers from Texas. When they finally caught up with me here they decided to settle and bought a ranch, and they've pretty much bought the town. Plenty of money again, they don't need mine. Just want revenge, I think. Black Creek belongs to the Dagetts. To keep the hotel, I was forced into an agreement that if things went well for them I would marry one of them after a couple of years. I had no choice but to agree. Maybe if I'd given in to them down in Texas. . . . So they're always watching me. I had to choose one of them, and now they're insisting on it.

'They've done well for themselves, but in a crooked way. There isn't a single money-making racket going on in the Creek that isn't controlled by the Dagetts. They deal exclusively in corruption and intimidation. Ranching is just a front to look honest. They own virtually everything except my hotel. Bart told me all about their illegal trade in Texas. They were part of a ruthless gang of outlaws. Now Bull will run for mayor and win. He'll appoint Bart as the sheriff. We'll all become very wealthy and live happily ever after. Ha! I don't think so. Last year Bull had a riding accident. He's very bitter because he knows I would've chosen him.'

'Surely you couldn't marry his good-for-nothing brother. You want something better, don't you?'

'Yes . . . no . . . I don't know what I want. It was all going along well enough. But it's come to a head, they're pressing me. I don't have much choice. Then you turned up, and well . . . I know it's corny, but I just felt you could offer me something better.'

'That's not surprising. Anything might seem better under the circumstances.'

'No, it's more than that, Chace. Call it a woman's intuition!' she smiled at him. 'You are interested, aren't you? I mean, a few moments ago you said. . . .'

Chace felt himself blush from his neck to the roots of his hair, and he couldn't find any words.

Bryony leant over and kissed him on the cheek, 'You don't have to say it. Ooh, that was painful.' She put her hand to the corner of her mouth. 'It still stings. I need to sleep, Chace. See me into the bedroom.'

He helped her off the chaise longue and carried her

through the doorway into her velvet and silk-festooned boudoir. He eased her on to the bed.

'Chace, would you do me a favour? Bart was very upset when he left and he said he'd be back to sort me out. Would you sleep on the *chaise longue* in case he does? Just help me out of this dress first, please.'

'I ought to go back to my own room. If Bart finds out I've spent the night here, won't that make things worse?'

'Maybe, but I'd rather be safe.'

'What am I supposed to do, shoot him?'

'It won't come to that,' she assured him.

At that very moment, under cover of the night, Bart Dagett was mounting up with one of the ranch hands, having agreed with Bull as to how they were going to deal with the arrival of a bounty hunter who seemed to know too much. The two riders set off at an unhurried pace heading for Vendel's Hotel. In Bart's saddlebag was a length of strong hangman's rope and a makeshift hood.

Chace woke suddenly. It was pitch black and very cold. It felt like four in the morning, but he couldn't be sure. He could hear a clock ticking in the room, but it was too dark to see the time. He'd fallen asleep under a thick blanket that had slipped off in the night, and the drop in temperature had woken him. It was always coldest around this time before dawn. For a moment he thought he was in his own room, but he couldn't hear Jamie's gentle sleeping noises. Then he remembered where he was. First off, he felt his way round the room to check doors hadn't been opened while he was asleep. He thought he ought to check on Bryony and make sure she was all right.

His eyes gradually became accustomed to the dark as he felt his way through to Bryony's boudoir. The faintest glimmer of light came through a gap in the curtains. The bed covers were partly off and he pulled them over so she wouldn't wake from the cold air. She stirred and turned on her side. He wanted to lean down and kiss her, but he was afraid to disturb her, and anyway wouldn't take advantage of her being asleep. Satisfied that everything was all right, he went back to the chaise longue, stretched himself out and pulled the blanket over. He was asleep again within minutes. The next time he woke, the sun was streaming in.

He rubbed his eyes. Seven o'clock had gone, but eight hadn't yet arrived. Cook would be busy doing breakfasts down in the hotel kitchen, and the barkeep would be sweeping the saloon ready for the day's trade to begin. Maids would be getting ready to clean the rooms, change the bed linen and take things to the town laundry. Chace didn't want anyone to see him coming down from Bryony's suite, fuelling idle gossip. He went through the side room to the fire-escape door. He eased it open, and making sure nobody was about, went quickly and silently down the steps. Once down, he sauntered off towards the livery corral to pass a bit of time and check on the horses.

The sky was beginning to cloud over and the early morning sun looked a little shaky. Parts of the town were slowly coming to life as blinds went up, shutters opened, and merchandise was brought out on to the boardwalks. Having checked on the horses, Chace went back to the hotel. He went in through the saloon batwings and was about to order a coffee, but the barkeep spoke first.

'Ah, Mr Hexx, I'm glad I've seen you. There was a note for you on the counter this morning.'

'A note?'

'Yes, it's behind the reception desk.'

They went through into the hotel, the barkeep got the note from under the desk, handed the folded paper to Chace and went back into the saloon.

Chace slid his finger under the seal and unfolded the paper. He read it through, paused, and read it again. Then he folded the paper, put it in his pocket and rushed up the stairs two at a time to the top floor. He knocked lightly on Bryony's door, and when there was no reply, went straight in. Fearing the worst, he opened the door to her bed chamber and was taken aback to see her serenely lying under the covers. But the noise had disturbed her, and her eyelids flickered a couple of times before opening wide.

'Chace? Is it morning already?'

He heaved a sigh of relief and sat down on the edge of the bed. 'It is, and I'm mighty glad to see you're still here.'

Her eyes remained half closed and her brow furrowed. 'What?'

'I thought you might have been kidnapped. Taken hostage or something.'

She frowned. 'You wanted to be rid of me?'

'No, I'm serious. Somebody left a note for me downstairs saying if I wanted you back alive I'd have to take ten thousand dollars in cash to the Dagetts' ranch.'

Bryony sat up. 'What are you talking about?'

He took the note out of his pocket and opened it up. She took it from him.

'I don't understand,' she said. 'You shouldn't go, they'll just shoot you. But why send a note and tell you to take ten thousand dollars to have me released when I'm still here?'

'They must have come in the night, but somehow knew

you weren't alone and didn't want to risk gunplay. It was a good thing you asked me to stay.'

'But you would have heard them. Unless . .' she paused.

'Unless what?'

'Chace, let me see the note. It says to deliver the money tonight to release the hostage. Maybe it never was me. . . .'

'Jamie!' exclaimed Chace. He leapt up from the bed and ran down the stairs to his own apartment, where his worst nightmare was confirmed. The washstand had been knocked over, the smashed basin lying on the floor. Jamie's bed was empty, his check shirt and corduroy trousers still on the chair. Chace ran straight back up the stairs to Bryony's suite with the news.

'We'll have to get across to Sheriff Lowe and tell him what's happened,' Bryony decided quickly.

'No,' said Chace, emphatically. 'This is personal. It's about me, not you. How could they know? What did you tell Bart about me? Did you mention Tom Purdy? You must have. It's always the same, one thing leads to another, one crime gives birth to another, and each time the monster gets bigger and bigger until it becomes so big you don't even see it.' He paused, eyes blazing with anger. 'Last night I might have walked away from all this. I didn't want to involve you, it's really my battle for Tom Purdy and justice.'

'You think the Dagetts were responsible for your friend's death?'

'No, not exactly, but things have come full circle. Now I see how it all adds up. Unfortunately you've complicated things. There's something between you and me, an attraction we can't ignore, a damn rope that binds us more tightly each time we see each other. I know how you feel,

Bryony, because I feel the same way about you. There ain't no explaining it. It just happens. But now the Dagetts have made the biggest mistake of their lives, because there's one person I value above Tom right now, and that's because he hasn't got any choices. Jamie isn't an independent human being, and I'm responsible for him.'

Bryony took advantage of the pause. 'That boy's thirteen, he's a fine lad, well built, tall, good looking, and with his head screwed on. He's as near independent as he ever will be. According to what you said, when his pa died he turned his back on his family, choosing you instead. Why? Because you were his safe ticket to a new life. Never mind the horses you've given him, they're a bonus. He made the decision to go with you because he is already more independent than you realize. The reason you feel responsible for him is because you want to. Because you want to care for someone other than yourself. Maybe he's made you grow up, too.'

'Wow, that's hard hitting,' Chace declared, reeling from the words.

'It's the way a woman hits hardest, with her tongue. Now, Chace Hexx, what are you goin' to do about this situation?'

It was a good question. Chace spent the day mooching around Black Creek figuring the best way to tackle the problem. It had to be resolved for good, and that carried a whole heap of risk. He let it be known that he was needing to take money out of the bank. It wasn't a problem getting the money, he had more than what was needed. He had deposited exactly ten thousand dollars in the bank when they came to Black Creek, and the rest he had stashed away in his room, just in case the bank got robbed! It was obvious there was a line of communication between someone in the bank and the Dagetts. How else would they demand the exact amount? That wasn't surprising in view of what Bryony had told him. The Dagetts owned everything in Black Creek, but Chace didn't plan to pay them one single penny piece. He had to withdraw the money or they would know he wasn't going to pay up. It was important to look as if he had every intention of paying.

Chace wondered if it wouldn't be easier to go and see Sheriff Lowe and get some legal backing. But how, and whom could he trust? There was only one person to trust, and that was Bryony. She had nothing to gain by kidnapping Jamie. But then it occurred to him, if he hadn't been staying with her, they couldn't have taken the boy. Come to think of it, he hadn't inspected her for bruises or anything, just that small cut inside her mouth, which she could have done by biting her cheek. Faking unconsciousness is easy. Had he been the victim of a simple set-up? Perhaps Bryony was so afraid of the Dagetts that she was going along with a plan to eliminate this bounty hunter who seemed hell bent on avenging Tom Purdy. She'd certainly gained his trust very easily with her feminine wiles.

Late in the afternoon Chace went across to the bank to collect his money. He was well aware why the Dagetts had chosen night time for the handover. Nobody would notice when his room was cleared out and the horses quietly removed from livery. Both he and Jamie were about to be brushed off the face of the earth.

He ate a large plate of steak and beans for dinner, and drank just two glasses of beer. He wanted a full belly but a steady hand. Outside, the setting sun's gold edging was fading from the rim of the clouds. The threatening storm had passed off to the north without hitting Black Creek. Chace loaded up his weapons – a pocket pistol in one boot, a knife in the other, a six-gun in his holster and a Winchester in the scabbard. All of these might be useful, but his insurance came in the form of Bryony, coerced to ride with him. The Dagetts weren't the only ones to have a hostage for bargaining.

Chace pressed his heels into the pinto, and with Bryony on another horse roped to his saddle, they set off for the ride to the Dagett ranch along a road that was just visible, partly illuminated by the crescent moon.

13

Chace had misgivings about taking Bryony to the Dagett ranch. He insisted she might go along in case anything went badly wrong, and she might be able to help, intervene in the negotiations. After all, if Bart Dagett wanted to marry her he'd surely listen to her, wouldn't he? Bryony was reluctant, and Chace couldn't guarantee which side she would help. He wanted to believe that if she had to choose, she would now side with him, unless she was playing a very dangerous game. It was a chance he'd have to take.

They were not more than fifteen minutes up the north road when he changed his mind and pulled up. The rope brought Bryony's horse to a stop.

'Look,' he said, 'I want to be honest with you. Something's bothering me. There's going to be trouble and I don't want you hurt.'

'I know,' she said straightaway. 'Me too. I don't want you to walk into a trap.'

'A trap?'

'Yes, I know how they think. If the Dagetts want something, they'll get it. Right now they probably believe you're a bounty hunter from Texas. They'll kill you for sure, and Jamie. And probably me too, because they think I'm helping you.'

Chace could only see the whites of her eyes in the moonlight, but he could tell she was serious.

'But . . . Bart wants to marry you.'

Bryony heaved a big sigh. 'No, he doesn't. He's just a go-between. Bull still insists on marrying me. He'll take control of the hotel and everything, including me. He wants me to stand next to him when he runs for mayor, it'll look better if he has a wife. Once he's elected, and legally owns the hotel by marriage, he won't want anything more to do with me. I always knew it was just a matter of time. Now they're close to having everything they want, and it doesn't include me. One dark night I'll be disposed of. They're not nice people, just out for themselves.'

'I guess I'm no different, really,' said Chace with a shrug.

'Oh yes you are,' Bryony asserted, reaching across and putting her hand on his arm. 'Everything you've done shows you want to make something good out of your life. You're decent and honest. You've got a conscience. Let's dismount a moment and I'll tell you why I agreed to come along.'

They dismounted under the pines, dark and quiet.

'For the last two years, the Dagetts have been waiting for an opportunity to take the hotel business away from me. That's all they want, just to get even because I stole their money. Everything went bad for them in Texas, they had to leave in a hurry, which is why they came after me. I'm just a cashbox and a piece of real estate. They don't care about me as a person. I've dreamt a dozen ways I could get rid of them. All those dreams again. But it's not that easy, they're too well established, Bull's a big noise round here. If I tried anything, they'd hear about it before I'd even finished thinking it through.'

'This is beginning to sound a bit familiar,' Chace remarked, heavily. 'That's how they knew about my money.'

They were both silent for a moment. A bird flapped off a nearby branch and flew away in the dark. A startled raccoon scurried through the undergrowth, and the tree-tops swished gently in the night breeze. Their eyes became more accustomed to the lack of light, and in the stillness they found themselves looking into each other's soul. Bryony put her arms round Chace's neck and planted her lips fair and square on his before he realized what she was doing. He melted, and they remained in a warm embrace, almost afraid to let go, lest the moment couldn't be regained.

'That's why I came with you. You and me, Chace, we have a life ahead of us. Heaven knows how we come to be here together like this in the dark, standing under a clump of trees, but it just feels as if this is the way it's meant to be. Don't you feel the same, Chace Hexx?'

He didn't know what to say. For the moment he was trying to reconcile two conflicting thoughts. On the one hand he couldn't ignore the pleasure of what had just happened, while on the other, everything seemed to be playing into Bryony's hands. Was she using him, or was she truly wanting him? Chace had laid out all his chips, then suddenly realized Bryony was holding four aces. Should he call, check, or throw in his cards?

'Yes, I do feel the same, so you must go back. I have no

intention of giving them any money. I'm going to get Jamie, and that's all there is to it.'

She broke away from him and mounted up. 'I thought so. And you can't send me away that easily.' She untied her horse from his saddle. 'You don't need a rope to keep me with you. You're stuck with me, like it or not.'

Chace knew there was no point in arguing once her mind was made up. He climbed on to the pinto and they regained the road. Bryony's declaration, and his acceptance, had changed everything: the past was discarded, the future stretched out before them – but the present still had to be faced.

The remaining distance to the ranch seemed to take hardly any time at all. They dropped off the main track and made their way carefully and quietly through the forest fringe. Chace figured the Dagetts might have posted a lookout on the road. He was anxious to keep his arrival quiet, and to stake out the lie of the land. He wished he'd been able to look over the ranch when he'd come out with Jamie. Now it was going to be more difficult guessing where he was hidden.

Chace turned to Bryony. 'I want you to wait here. . . .'

'Give me your hat,' Bryony demanded.

'What? My hat, why?'

Before he could protest, she had reached across and removed his hat. She put her heels into her horse and moved off before Chace could stop her.

'Hey! Where are you going. . . ?' But she was already beyond the range of his loud whisper. He urged the pinto forwards cautiously until he could just see Bryony's outline going down into the Bar BBD yard. Wearing his hat, and silhouetted against the night sky, it was impossible to tell it wasn't him.

148

'Oh, Jeez!' Chace exclaimed, suddenly realizing what she was doing. But before he could decide what to do about it, a shot rang out, and horrified, he watched Bryony fall from the horse.

'We got him!' came the shout from the yard. 'Plumb dead!'

Chace's instinct was to run across and attend to Bryony, but two men with a lantern came out from one of the buildings. Chace slid off the pinto, wrapped the reins round a branch, snatched the Winchester from the scabbard and lay low while the two figures came running up the track. With their guns drawn, the two men quickly made their way towards the point where Bryony had fallen. The swinging light kept flashing across the men's faces but neither of them was Bart Dagett, and Chace hadn't met Bull to know what he looked like. He suspected they were two ranch hands positioned ready to murder Chace when he showed up. It was exactly what he had tried to avoid, and because of her rash stupidity, they'd shot Bryony instead. When she fell to the ground, the horse had reared and made off into the undergrowth, there was no sign of it.

Soon on the spot, and not more than fifty yards from where Chace was crouching in the undergrowth, the two men started scuffing around at the edge of the track.

'Where is the sonofabitch?' said one. 'He must've fallen 'bout here.'

Chace watched them searching with the lantern, then the ranch-house door opened down in the yard and the light outlined a figure in the doorway. A voice called up, 'Have you got him there?' It sounded very much like Bart Dagett.

'Shot him all right,' was the shouted reply. 'Winged

him good, but he's wriggled into the scrub. There's blood on the track where he fell, but it's difficult to follow in the dark.'

Chace was heartened by the fact that Bryony wasn't dead, but he didn't know how badly she might be injured.

Bart Dagett shouted back, 'Well, find him quick and bring him down here.' He went inside and closed the door. It opened again almost at once. 'Bull says if he's dead we can get rid of the boy.' The door was slammed shut.

One of the searchers spoke into the dark. 'You hear that, Hexx? If you're dead the boy gets it too. If you're alive you'd better give yourself up.'

Chace knew he needed to find Bryony as soon as he could. While the shouting was going on, he had slipped away from the pinto and hidden further off up the track.

'Up here. . . .' he said in a weak voice but just loud enough to be heard, then he crept another twenty yards further away as the two figures moved towards him. 'I'm shot bad,' he mumbled. He heard the guns being cocked at the ready, but they still couldn't find him.

'Show yourself,' said one of the searchers. 'Where are you, Hexx?'

'Right here,' whispered Chace into the man's ear from behind, bringing the butt of his six-gun crashing down on the man's skull. He fell to the ground with a loud moan. The other man carrying the lantern hadn't the time to do anything before Chace had the barrel of his gun pressed into his temple, and said 'Drop the gun!'

The man let the gun fall from his hand. Chace took the lantern from him and held it to his face. 'Put 'em up high and keep 'em there.'

'It wasn't my idea, mister, I just do what I'm told. I was told to shoot you soon as you rode down that path.'

'Tell me who's inside the house.'

'The Dagetts and a couple ranch hands.'

'And the boy?'

'I ain't sayin'.'

'Anyone guarding him?'

'Maybe.'

Chace smacked the man's jaw with the revolver – he didn't feel inclined to be gentle with someone who had just tried to kill him. 'How many?'

The man gasped, wincing at the pain in his mouth. 'Easy up, mister!'

'Speak,' Chace demanded, threatening to smack him again.

The man cowered. 'The boy's tied up and you won't find him easy. You don't stand a chance, mister.'

'Neither do you,' said Chace, and this time he hit him so hard under the chin his knees gave way instantly.

Going to the pinto as quickly as he could, Chace retrieved rope and tied the two unconscious men together, binding their legs and using their own bandanas as gags.

He called out as loud as he dared. 'Bryony! Bryony!' But there was no answer.

Maybe she was unconscious through blood loss. He used the lantern to find where she had fallen off the horse, the blood was still red and wet but he couldn't follow any trail. At least it seemed she wasn't losing too much. He called her name again, but still no reply. Just then the ranch-house door opened again.

There was no mistaking Bart Dagett. 'Have you found him, Amos?'

Chace muffled his voice, held the lantern as low as possible and tried to imitate the voice he'd heard earlier. 'I got him all right, he's here, I need a hand to carry him.'

'Where's Mulley?'

'Dunno,' Chace continued, imitating. 'I need a hand.' He hoped Dagett wouldn't come up himself, but would send up one or both of the pokes from the house.

Then the bunkhouse door opened and a figure came out carrying a rifle. 'What's going on, Mr Dagett?'

'Don't worry Micah, get back in with the boy. Amos has got Hexx up on the track.' Dagett went back into the doorway and summoned one of the cowpokes from the ranch-house. 'Get up there, Nat, and give Amos a hand with Hexx.'

Nat came out and closed the door.

Chace swung the lantern as a signal. 'Up here, Nat.'

'I can't see too good, my eyes aren't accustomed to the dark yet.'

'Here.' Chace put the lantern down on the track as a marker and slid into the scrub. Just before Nat reached the lantern, Chace called him over.

'He's here,' Chace said. Then suddenly taking full advantage of the dark he launched a surprise attack. Springing out of the scrub he struck Nat a shattering blow before he knew what had hit him.

With three men down, the odds were beginning to go in his favour, and by chance, he now knew where they were holding Jamie. Chace was torn. Where in tarnation was Bryony? If she had crawled away and was lying somewhere injured he had to find her. A small amount of blood didn't necessarily mean she wasn't hurt bad. But now that the ranch was alerted to the fact that Chace had been captured and was apparently being taken down to the ranch house, he had to act quickly. His first priority was Jamie, and there was no time to bind and gag Nat.

Making his way quickly down the track Chace was soon outside the bunkhouse. He tapped lightly on the door, 'Micah! Micah!'

In a moment the door opened and a head popped out. 'Yeah?'

Smack! Chace's fist met him between the eyes and Micah staggered back into the room. Pushing past the pole-axed body, Chace started searching the bunks in the light of a guttering candle. 'Jamie! Jamie! It's me, Chace.' He whispered as loudly as he dared. A muffled noise came from the furthest corner. Chace found the boy under a blanket, tied and gagged. He pulled the gag off.

Jamie stretched his jaw, 'Am I glad. . . .'

'No time to talk,' Chace said, clamping his hand over Jamie's mouth like another gag. The boy's eyes widened at the sudden closing of his jaw. 'Listen carefully, Jamie. Get back up the track and search around for my pinto, whistle him like I do and he'll snort, he's tied up on the left side, fifty yards off the track. If you find him, get on him and ride back to Sheriff Lowe. Tell him to get a posse together and get out here fast.'

He cut through the binding ropes on Jamie's arms and legs, ushered him to the door, looked out to check all was clear and pushed him off into the night. 'Now get going!'

Using the rope from Jamie's bindings, Chace secured Micah's body and lugged him across the room to the bunk where Jamie had been. He laid him on the bed and covered him over. He left the bunkhouse and slithered across to the ranch house. Peering through a window, he was looking into a darkened dining room. Through a doorway on the far side, he could see only lamp-light and shadows. Surely it wouldn't be long before they realized something had gone wrong with Amos, Mulley and Nat, and why they hadn't yet returned with Chace's body.

He waited and watched, wondering if Jamie had found the pinto. He crept back beside the bunkhouse, and other thoughts came flooding into his mind. The Dagetts had planned to kill him and Jamie. If he came out of this mess alive, he wasn't going to spend the rest of his life looking over his shoulder. This had to be the last time. His future not only included Jamie, but could include Bryony as well. If Bull Dagett became mayor and his brother became sheriff, the citizens of Black Creek would be subjected to endless corruption and intimidation. Chace couldn't take on all these problems by himself. What about the ranch hands? He'd tied up three of them, Nat was free but out cold, and there was still one inside. He couldn't with good conscience kill innocent ranch hands who were simply acting under orders. While wrestling with that dilemma, the situation all sparked off.

'Mr Dagett! I've been jumped. The sonofabitch is loose out here.'

It was Nat calling out and very groggy, running helter-skelter down the track. Chace had no time to decide, instinct kicked in. He levelled the Winchester as Nat came into the yard and fired just one shot, which knocked him off balance and dropped him to the ground. The door to the ranch house was flung open and Bart Dagett stood there with his gun drawn. Nat called out a warning, pointing towards Chace. Dagett shot off two hopeful rounds in

Chace's direction. The lead thudded into the bunkhouse timbers. Silhouetted by the light, Dagett was an easy target. Chace's Winchester spat fire. With a sickening thud, Bart Dagett's chest was shattered; he gasped his last breath and fell by the doorway. Now, as far as he knew, there were just two more men inside, Bull Dagett and a ranch hand.

Suddenly a window was flung open and a shot came flashing into the night. He'd been spotted from inside the ranch house. Shadows flickered, but he couldn't catch sight of anyone. Minutes passed and nothing more happened. Someone was waiting for him to make a move.

Chace made a snap decision. He leapt up and rushed to the ranch house, burst through the door and fired two wild shots from his handgun as he took cover beside a table. After the initial burst of energy and the element of surprise, Chace was himself surprised to see two figures at the further end of the room, one standing, the other sitting. The man standing was clearly the ranch hand, and he had a rifle pointing in Chace's direction. The man sitting down must be Bull Dagett. Chace flicked his eyes towards him momentarily, not wanting to lose sight of the trigger finger on the rifle pointing in his direction.

Bull Dagett spoke calmly and with authority: 'Hello, Mr Hexx.' He turned to his ranch hand. 'Hal, put up your gun, there's no need for that. Mr Hexx isn't going to shoot either of us. He's only come for the boy, and we'll let him have the boy.'

Ranch-hand Hal holstered his gun. Chace turned his attention to Bull. That was when he saw the blanket across his knees, his hands pinned under the blanket and the chair with its two big wheels either side. Bull Dagett was sitting in a wheelchair.

'I haven't come just for the boy. Does the name Tom Purdy mean anything to you?' Chace took the brass star out of his pocket. 'Do you know what this is? The Rees brothers, Heyman, Nickleson, those names mean something?'

Bull Dagett narrowed his eyes. 'So you are a bounty hunter. Bryony said she thought you were. I don't suppose you brought the ransom money, did you?'

Chace's head started spinning, this wasn't at all what he had expected, but it suddenly explained a lot of things. The riding accident for one. Was this incapable cripple Bryony's nemesis, the monster she had to be rid of? The man who would use her and toss her aside? Or was this the man she really planned to marry? He sat there as cool as snowmelt, assured, relaxed, reasonable. How was Chace going to bring him to justice? Bull Dagett knew he was untouchable.

'Is Bart dead?' Bull asked.

'I dunno,' Chace lied.

'And the others?'

'Tied up except Nat, who's lying outside, shot in the leg.'

This was almost a normal kind of conversation. The kind you have in a nightmare. Chace was losing his grip on reality. He lowered his gun and walked towards them. It was a bad miscalculation.

There was a deafening *bang!* as a bullet tore through the blanket and ripped into the side of Chace's leg. Without a second thought, Chace drew lightning fast and returned the shot. The wheelchair took off backwards, crashing into the wall. Hal swung round, his attention drawn to the big red stain spreading across Bull Dagett's chest. Chace's gun was now pointing squarely at Hal. 'Put 'em up!' was all he said. The cowpoke put his hands in the air. Chace relieved him of his hand gun and made Hal check Bull's pulse. There wasn't one.

Trying to ignore the pain in his thigh, while pressing his bandanna into the wound to stop the bleeding, Chace took Hal, hands high, into the yard to tend to Nat. As they stepped outside Sheriff Lowe came down the track with a posse of a half-dozen men. At the back, Chace could see a boy on a pinto.

'Have you seen Bryony?' were Chace's first words to the sheriff.

'She's being patched up by the doc. Came back into town shouting for me. She wanted to come back here, but I wouldn't let her. She ain't badly shot, a graze, but it needs a couple stitches. Shortly afterwards your boy arrived and we got the posse together. What's the situation here?'

What indeed was the situation? Chace had no idea. He'd suppressed the pain as long as he could, but fainted clean away before he could make any answer.

Bar BBD in Black Creek has been renamed by the new owner. It's still a prosperous cattle ranch; the buildings have been extended and more land added. The previous owner and his brother are buried in the town cemetery. The ranch hands from the old Bar BBD are serving long sentences in the county penitentiary for aiding and abetting the kidnapping of a minor. One of them, Hal Holt by name, had his sentence reduced for giving evidence at the trial, and asserting that the shooting of Bull Dagett was an act of self-defence, Bull having fired first. The jury had agreed, and judged the same was true of Bart. Chace Hexx had walked free from court.

157

About four hundred miles away from Black Creek to the north-west in Butte Falls, Montana, a big spread by the name of The Star H, was already raising five hundred head of cattle. Run by a man and his wife with the help of a couple of ranch hands and a young lad, they were new settlers. It was inaccurately rumoured the man was a former bounty hunter from somewhere down south, but they never saw him wearing a gun-belt. His wife apparently used to own a hotel in Colorado. It was also rumoured, also inaccurately, that she might open another one in Butte Falls to bring more tourists and trade to the area. Actually, they had both embraced a fresh start and had put the past where it belonged. The truth was that they were blissfully happy in their new life.

The boy, Jamie, had multiplied those seven horses threefold and has an adequate part of the ranch to graze and breed. He keeps saying one day he'll have a spread of his own, but he doesn't yet seem inclined to break away. Maybe fifteen is a bit young to go out on his own, or maybe he just likes Bryony's home cooking too much to leave.

And now there's another boy on the way. At least Chace likes to think so. He's already decided to call it Tom, if it is male, or maybe Tommie if not. It's due any time soon, and the nursery in the ranch house has been decked out ready for the new baby. Chace made the pinewood crib himself from his own trees on the ranch, spending long hours mastering tricky turning and carving techniques. He cussed a bit when intricate detailing broke off, but that was more than made up for by the pleasure of the productive cycle. The wood grew on his own land, he harvested it, seasoned it, and had lovingly manufactured a useful item from it. The same was true of the cycle of beef production. It gave him immense satisfaction. And now he was about to raise his own family, too. What more could a man want?

It was a warm summer's evening; there was a gentle breeze rustling the long grass. The deliciously delicate aroma of the climbing roses drifted across the veranda. Chace and Bryony were sitting side by side on the swing seat, his arm around her shoulders, his hand stroking her bump.

'D'you know, Chace, never in a thousand years could I have imagined this.'

He continued stroking the bump.

She smiled at him and put her hand on top of his. 'You, the ranch, Jamie, everything. And now our first baby. I never knew I could feel so content. And hey! You never have told me why we called this place The Star H.'

'Really not? Well, there's the mystery.'

'Tell me,' she demanded, prodding him in the ribs.

'Well, the H is for you and me of course, Chace and Bryony Hexx.'

She turned to him, 'I always meant to ask you, Hexx is a strange name, I mean two x's.'

'It had one originally I believe, but my pa couldn't write and when he signed a document once with an 'x' he put it next to the Hex that the lawyer had written, and so it became Hexx. That's what I was told, anyway.'

'And now The Star H.'

'Yes, the star, that's how it all started. A simple brass star, stolen and recovered. Tom's Ranger star. It's what set me on a worthwhile path. Sometimes you can make a new life, sometimes you can't. It's whether you have the strength to move on. It's what you do from here on that matters, not what's done and dusted.' He pulled Bryony awkwardly across the seat and kissed her tenderly full on the mouth.

'Mind the baby!' she exclaimed.

'Yeah, yeah,' Chace laughed. 'Mind the baby!'